I0517132

Theaker's Quarterly Fiction #54

Edited by
Stephen Theaker
and John Greenwood

Theaker's Quarterly Fiction #54

Edited by
Stephen Theaker
and John Greenwood

Cover Artist

Howard Watts

Contributors

Charles Wilkinson
Douglas J. Ogurek
Jacob Edwards
Patrick Whittaker

Contents

Editorial

Fiction

The Quarterly Review

Reviews by Stephen Theaker, Douglas J. Ogurek and Jacob Edwards

Audio

Books

Comics

Editorial

Stephen Theaker

This Issue

Once more I must apologise to our readers and our contributors for the delay in this issue's publication. It's not quite so late as issue fifty-three, but we had planned to bring it out in December. I hope the two superb stories and all the reviews in this issue will make it up to you. If not, maybe the next four issues we publish this year will do the trick.

First, we have an entire novella for you by Patrick Whittaker, "The Policeman and the Silence". I won't say too much about the story, because, as ever, I like you to discover everything for yourselves, but it's hardboiled, fantastical, and mysterious. I encouraged him to submit it elsewhere before letting us publish it, but he declined, and so here it is. Count yourselves lucky.

Secondly, there is "Septs", a long story by Charles Wilkinson, quickly becoming one of my favourite short story writers. Each one is different, and yet they're all so good. This one came to us as part of a kind of exchange programme. I was helping out on *BFS Horizons* #2, realised we had a story from Charles, "Catapedamania", in the TQF subs folder that would round it out perfectly, and asked if I could use it there. Charles agreed, but pointed out that "Septs" had been waiting in the *BFS Horizons* submissions pile, so we brought it over here. Turnabout is fair play.

And then we have another massive review section. Jacob Edwards and Douglas Ogurek both offer their takes on the new Star Wars film (I liked it very much too). Jacob also reviews *Savages* by K.J. Parker, *The Shepherd's Crown* by Terry Pratchett and *Stoker's Manuscript* by Royce Prouty, while Douglas also reviews *Goosebumps*, *The Green Inferno*, *The Hunger Games: Mockingjay, Part 2*, *Krampus* and *The Visit*. I review too much to list here, but rather less skillfully than my colleagues!

I hope you enjoy it. See you again in March for our special themed issue, edited by our magnificent cover artist Howard Watts.

Double Standards

Part of the fallout from the Spectral Press collapse, which looked worse the longer things went on, was that one review site declared that it would no longer accept books from small presses that don't pay contributors. Seems fair, you might think, whatever, it's up to them how they filter their bookload. However, they went on to say that people who publish stuff without paying contributors are "despicable", and that if you can't pay your contributors you shouldn't be publishing at all. Those aren't unusual views, especially in the US, where people like Nick Mamatas have been particularly vocal about the need to pay contributors, and extremely hostile, unsurprisingly, to those journals that are beginning to charge writers to even have their submissions considered. What made this announcement a bit peculiar – and you've probably already guessed where this is going – is that it came from a review site that doesn't pay its own contributors. It was a publisher who doesn't pay contributors saying that publishers who don't pay their contributors are despicable.

The site owner and contributors explained that it's okay for them not to pay contributors because their blog is a labour of love, a non-profit. I agree, I don't see a problem with that. But why them, and not other publishing projects run on exactly the same basis? If that approach is okay for them, why would they would label *Theaker's Quarterly Fiction*, *Holdfast*, *Fur-Lined Ghettos*, *BFS Horizons*, *Vector* and so many other interesting, non-commercial little publishing projects despicable? One of the site's contributors reckoned that the site "isn't a publisher", it's all "squarely for the benefit of the publishers and writers", which is a slightly odd way to approach reviewing, but I think it comes down to a bit of double thinking that is quite common, whereby fiction writers are treated with a kind of holy reverence, and must be paid, while payment of non-fiction writers, reviewers in particular, is optional.

I've even heard people suggest that the book itself is payment for a reviewer. I don't buy it. Writing is writing. Work is work. What paperback could ever stand as payment for ten or twenty hours of your time? If you don't think *everyone* should be paid for their writing, you've implicitly accepted that there are situations in which it's okay to publish writing without paying for it. We may disagree about what those situations are, but you definitely can't claim the moral high ground if you aren't paying anyone either.

There are people out there who are working extremely hard to make their small presses profitable enough to pay their contributors, and they have our immense admiration. There are people publishing uncommercial projects who pay contributors out of their own pockets to make them happen, and they have our admiration too. But we think there's a place in the world for non-commercial projects, that don't make any money, that don't take any money, that are purely created for fun, as a hobby.

Having said that, I found the advice of the wisest man in the world, Judge John Hodgman in the case of "Go Set a Tip Jar", quite compelling. He talked there about charging a bit for projects, however small, both to encourage people to recognise their value, and to enable you to give them more attention, to invest more time in them. Definitely gave me something to think about. I doubt that will lead to us charging for this magazine, but we might be a bit more forward about saying, if you enjoyed this free magazine, why not thank our contributors by buying one of their books?

Books Read in 2015

Now, this may not interest everyone, so don't feel bad if you want to skip it and move onto the stories and reviews. No one will blame you: this look back at my reading in 2015 will interest me if no one else. I read 165 books during 2015, according to my Goodreads list. (That sounds a lot, but read on: there were a lot of comics and very short books.) That includes some that I began in previous years, but it also leaves out some that I started in 2015 but didn't finish, so it all evens out. I bought 130 of the books I read, 17 were review copies, 8 were gifts, 5 were books I produced, and another 5 were borrowed.

I read 111 comics last year – graphic novels and trade paperbacks, that is, I'm not counting single issues. Dark Horse had a big Star Wars sale at the end of 2014 and I bought a lot of them. One book I read was a coffee table book (full-colour pictures of ZX Spectrum games; see review in this issue). 50 were prose books, five of them being books I produced for us or the BFS. So 45 prose books, which is still more than I'd have predicted.

152 of the books I read in 2015 were by men. 13 by women. That's pretty terrible. In 2014 it was 113 by men and 25 by women, so the percentage by women went down from 18% to 8%. That's partly down to reading lots and lots of comics by a handful of writers (3 out of the 111 comics I read were by women, compared to 9 out of 50 of the prose books, and 1 out of 3 audiobooks), but it's also because I wasn't making the effort I made in 2014 to alternate between reviewing prose books by men and women. Whatever the reason, it's disappointing!

To diversify my reading in 2016 I'm taking up a reading challenge set by my older daughter's school, where you have to read two books in each of twenty categories (crime, classics, romance, non-fiction, etc), using each author only once. To the school challenge's rules I've added my own, to read at most one male writer in each category. I've been enjoying the challenge, but it's embarrassing how hard I'm finding it to fill some slots with female writers from my collection, despite having thousands of books.

Anyway, back to 2015. My most read authors were: John Ostrander (10 books – the *Star Wars: Legacy* series), Robert Kirkman (9 – *The Walking Dead* and *Invincible*), Adam Warren (5 – *Empowered*), James Kochalka (4 – three of them *Johnny Boo* books for kids) and Mike Mignola (4 – all Hellboy spin-offs).

The publisher I read most of this year was once again Dark Horse, by a long, long way, thanks to all their sales, some in the run-up to losing the Star Wars licence and others after they finally joined Comixology: I read 46 of their books (up from 33 in 2014). Then 13 from Image, 11 from DC, 9 from Penguin, 7 from Subterranean and 4 from Top Shelf.

The longest prose book I read was *Killing Floor*, the first Jack Reacher novel, at 525pp. Not the kind of thing I'd review for this magazine, but it was enjoyable. Having read it, the casting of Tom Cruise as this human giant makes much more sense: the character may be big, but he's defined more by his determination and quick-thinking. *Tales of the Marvellous and News of the Strange* was shorter (but much more of a struggle to get through) at 496pp. The shortest was Vaughan Stanger's *None of Our Yesterdays* at 31pp.

The longest comic was a Commando collection, *The Dirty Dozen*, which was 775pp – took me years to finish that one! The shortest was *Johnny Boo: Twinkle Power* at 36pp.

In 2014 I gave five stars to five books, and in 2015 I was even more enthusiastic: eight books got five stars from me: *Usagi Yojimbo Saga, Vol. 1* by Stan Sakai, *Queen and Country: The Definitive Edition, Vol. 2* by Greg Rucka and chums, *God is Not Great: How Religion Poisons Everything* by Christopher Hitchens, *JLA, Vol. 1* by Grant Morrison and chums, *Usagi Yojimbo, Vol. 14: Demon Mask* by Stan Sakai, *Black Gods Kiss* by Lavie Tidhar, *The Glorkian Warrior and the Mustache of Destiny* by James Kochalka and *The Last Demon* by Isaac Bashevis Singer.

58 books got four stars, 77 got three stars, and 10 books got two stars. Just 1 book got one star: *Crystals R for Kids* by Leia A. Stinnett, a silly nonsense book that came free with some crystals one of the kids bought. My average rating for the books I read and rated this year was 3.4 (up from 3.23 the year before), while the average rating of Goodreads users for those books was 3.84 (not too different from 3.87 in 2014). There are some books I didn't rate: ones I worked on myself, obviously, but also stuff I'd read for review that wouldn't be out for a while.

I counted up how many books I read each month: January (16), February (7), March (28), April (9), May (16), June (9), July (18), August (6), September (7), October (9), November (4) and December (36). March was high because I read most of *Star Wars: Legacy*, a set of Subterranean Press novellas from a Humble Bundle, and a lot of the comics I got for my birthday. November was so low because I was trying to write a new novel: I try not to read anything when novel-writing so that I don't get distracted by writing reviews, or thinking about their stories instead of mine. Half of those read in December were on one day, December 31, when I spent almost an entire day reading comics. Bliss! (Would have read another two or three if we hadn't watched *Terminator Genisys*.)

All my reading added up (roughly – the page count isn't the most accurate part of the Goodreads database) to 34,863pp (up a lot from 27,125pp in 2014). The average length of the 50 prose books I read was 172pp (higher than I expected), coming to 8,635pp in total (down a little bit from 8,923pp in 2014). The average length of the comics read was 227pp (though as I remember that included an awful lot of sketchbook pages, alternate covers and the like), coming to 25,248pp in total (up a lot from 17,103pp in 2014). Averaging that out over the year, I read about 24pp a day of prose, and about 69pp a day of comics (three issues or so), amounting to 96pp a day when the audiobooks and a coffee table book are thrown in (up from 74pp a day in 2014). No wonder it took me so long to get TQF53 finished.

One odd thing, though I guess it didn't surprise me, was that while I read 165 books this year, I bought, received or acquired another 164 books that I haven't read yet (compared to 118 in 2014). From *Ancillary Sword* by Ann Leckie, added on January 22 (a review copy that I haven't finished listening to) through to

Asterix and the Missing Scroll, added on December 28 (we didn't open our Christmas presents till we got home from a trip to Yorkshire). That's a lot of overspill. I had as many books left over as I actually read. I now have 1,456 books to read (up from 1,348 last year), and 144 unfinished (up from 138 last year). It's getting worse not better! I don't need to buy any books this year, so I'm going to try not to. I think I'm long past the point where it starts to look like hoarding. But what a hoard to have.

Stephen Theaker*'s reviews have appeared in Interzone, Black Static, Prism and the BFS Journal, as well as clogging up our pages. He shares his home with three slightly smaller Theakers, runs the British Fantasy Awards, and works in legal and medical publishing.*

The Policeman and the Silence

Patrick Whittaker

---

1. Extermination

The kitchen floor trembled. I placed a glass of Kaza No. 3 whisky on the sideboard and observed how the liquid reacted to the passing of the subway train. It rose briefly up the side of the glass before cascading down to form a circular wave that collapsed in on itself only to blossom out again. As the rumbling beneath my feet intensified, all semblance of order in the glass vanished, leading to a very real danger of spillage. I had no option but to empty the glass down my throat.

Man, it was rough. Rough but friendly in a playful bulldog kind of way.

The train passed. Calm returned. I refreshed my glass and started thinking about breakfast.

A high window gave me a worm's eye view of the pavement running past my basement flat. A tuk-tuk spluttered by, its misfiring two-stroke engine putting me in mind of a 60-a-day smoker.

The phone rang. I grabbed the handset. "Seth Norton."

"There's been another one." The voice was gravel on sandpaper.

"A murder?"

"Nah. A bring and buy sale in aid of the local orphans. Of course a murder. Apartment 23, Montgolfier House, Rue Morgue. Get your arse over there as quick as you like."

As quick as I liked wasn't as quick as the Chief had in mind, but that was his look out. For one thing, I wasn't due back on duty for the best part of an hour. For another, I had no desire to examine a stiff on an empty stomach.

My frying pan was in the sink, a plateau crowning a mound of crockery and cutlery. Several flies and a smattering of bugs were held captive in a layer of congealed fat. Most were dead; the rest must have wished they were.

I checked the fridge. There was bacon, there were sausages. I had eggs and a half-full tin of baked beans. It was the makings of a decent breakfast.

The phone rang again. I took the bacon and the sausages and dumped them on the table. Then I back-heeled the fridge door and reached for the phone. "Seth Norton."

"You still there, Norton?"

"No, Chief. I left two minutes ago."

Compared to my hovel, Apartment 23, Montgolfier House was a palace. Compared to anywhere else, it was a hovel.

The late Citizen Anton Delgado lay face down on the living room carpet. He was wearing a pair of long johns and a stunned expression. Bits of the back of his head weren't where they should be. They were mostly on the carpet, though a few scraps clung to congealed blood on the poker that had apparently done for him.

"They remind me of mah-jongg tiles," said Citizen Gene Hooke, the police photographer. Careful not to disturb anything, he knelt beside the corpse to get a close up of the fatal wound. He took out his hanky and gingerly removed the spent flash bulb. Then he put bulb and hanky into his pocket before producing a fresh bulb which he fitted into the camera. "You ever play mah-jongg, Inspector?"

"Not really my sort of game."

"I'd have thought it right up your street. You being so cerebral and all that."

Citizen Gert Wyman overheard and barked a disdainful *hah!* "Cerebral, my arse. Loves to put on airs and graces, does our Detective Inspector Norton, but he doesn't fool me. I doubt he can even read."

"I can read you," I told him. "You fat toad."

It was an apt description. If I ever came across anything more toad-like than Wyman, I'd know for sure it was a toad.

He started the long, agonising business of removing his bulk from the armchair he was lounging in, then thought better of it. He didn't so much sit back down as drop like a sack in a laundry chute. "Six murders," he goaded. "Six murders and you haven't a clue about who's doing them."

"Seven."

"This one doesn't count. Whoever did this is a Johnny-Come-Lately – not the West Side Ripper. I'd have thought even a dunderhead like you could have figured that out."

"A murder's a murder. And the Ripper's a suspect until I decide otherwise."

"Come off it, Norton. All the Ripper's victims have been women. They've all come from the West Side and they've all been poisoned before having their internal organs harvested. Chummy here – in case you hadn't noticed – is clearly not a woman. He shows no sign of having been poisoned, and his innards are where his innards should be. Throw in the fact we're nowhere near the West Side and one can reasonably conclude there's a new killer in town."

"Conclude what you like, Wyman. I'll wait until I've a few more facts." I looked again at the hole in Delgado's skull. "Would I be right in saying the poker was driven into the victim's head?"

"With great force. Whoever did this is built like an ox – which clearly the West Side Ripper isn't."

"Who says he isn't?"

"I says he isn't. The sort of person who can remove internal organs with the precision of a skilled surgeon is not the sort who can conjure up enough brute force to drive a poker through someone's skull. Trust me: this is *not* the work of the Ripper."

I'd seen enough of the body and heard enough of Wyman. "I'm done here. When can I expect the pathology report?"

"When I'm good and ready to let you have it." Wyman heaved himself out of the chair – this time for real. The sweat stains under the armpits of his white jacket were wider and damper than usual, which prompted me to look up at the ceiling fan. It wasn't moving.

"What's up with the fan?" I asked.

Gene took another photograph of the corpse before answering. "Nothing. I turned it off."

"Now why would you do a thing like that?"

"I wanted to see old fatso sweat."

Wyman's face reddened. It looked like a tomato coated with morning dew. He swatted a switch on the wall. "If you ever end up in my morgue, they're going to bury you with your brains up your arse. You little pipsqueak!"

The ceiling fan went to work rendering the turgid air more breathable.

"You got all the photos you need?" I asked Gene.

"Not yet, Inspector. You're going to have to turn the body over so I can get him full frontal, as it were."

I make it a point to touch neither the dead nor the dying, so I motioned at the uniformed constable standing by the door. "Time for your good turn for the day."

The constable paled. "Me, Inspector? But I'm not trained for that sort of thing."

"Nobody is, son. Now if you don't mind..."

Giving me a look that could have curdled milk, the constable did as he was told before trotting off to the bathroom to empty his stomach.

The front of Anton Delgado's body was in better shape than the back. He was early fifties, slightly paunchy, cursed with a face like a gargoyle and most definitely dead.

"Right, I think I've seen enough." I pointed to a door. "Is that the study you were telling me about?"

"No," said Gene. "That's the bedroom."

"Where, if you remember," said Wyman, "a certain young lady is waiting to be questioned."

"She can wait," I said. "I want to see the study."

It wasn't my idea of a study. To me it looked like a workshop that happened to have a desk, a swivel chair and a book shelf. It also contained metal shelving packed with tools and machine parts, some of which looked familiar, some of which didn't.

Sergeant Studebaker had made himself at home in the swivel chair. He produced a rasping sound as he scratched his bristled chin. Square-jawed, swarthy, and forever looking like he was up to something, he was the sort you might not trust with your girlfriend but would be glad to have on your side if it came to fisticuffs. The first time I saw him, I knew he had to be a police sergeant. He was too much the type to be anything else.

"This guy," he declared, "was an A1 nutter. If he weren't dead, I'd have him sent off to the funny farm. I mean, take a look at this, will ya?"

From the desk he picked up a pocket watch and tossed it to me. With the slightest of fumbles, I managed to catch it.

It was a half hunter, which meant a glass panel on the outer lid did away with the need to open the case to tell the time. I had one like it, except the numbers on mine stopped at ten the way any sensible watch would.

This one went up to twelve.

"Twelve!" said Studebaker, in case I'd missed it. "What the fuck is that all about? And this?" He held up a ruler. "You see, boss? As well as centimetres, it's divided into something called inches – 12 in all. It's like this guy had a fetish for the number 12."

The desk was littered with tiny tools – the sort you'd expect to see in a jeweller's shop. There was also a soldering iron, an angle-poise lamp and a large magnifying glass.

I showed Studebaker the ID card I'd taken from Anton Delgado's jacket. "He is – or was – an engineer. Seems his work was also his hobby."

"Take a shufti at the back of that watch," Studebaker suggested "See if it doesn't give you goosebumps."

There was an inscription running around the edge of the watch. I had to use the magnifying glass on the desk to make out what it said. "*TAG Heuer. Switzerland.*" I could only shrug. "It's a bit cryptic but hardly the stuff of which goosebumps are made."

Studebaker took off his wrist watch and showed me its back. "You see that inscription? *K-Temp. North Side.* K-Temp being the manufacturer. North Side being where the K-Temp factory's located."

"So you think this was made by an outfit called TAG Heuer in some place called Switzerland?"

"Yeah, and neither of these things exist hereabouts. Now do you have goose bumps?"

"Not quite. But I'm getting there." If Studebaker was right, the watch must have come from Elsewhere. But then how had it ended up in Kaza-Blanka? "What about the ruler? Any indication as to where it was made?"

Studebaker put his watch back on. "You know, I didn't think to look." He picked up the ruler and examined the side with the markings. When that revealed nothing, he turned it over. "And there we have it. *Made in Hong Kong*. I ain't never heard of Hong Kong and I'd be willing to bet you ain't neither."

"OK, Sergeant. I now officially have goosebumps. You'd better bag the watch and ruler and see if you can find anything else that's out of place. While you're doing that, I'll have a chat with our witness."

The witness was in the bedroom, perched on the bed, blue jacket nestling on her shoulders, a uniformed constable in the chair beside her.

The first thing I noticed was how frail she seemed, how vulnerable. *Like a sparrow* I thought, remembering the time I'd held one in my hand and realised how easy it would be to crush the life out of it. What struck me next was that she had a killer body, eyes blazing with mischief and an elfin face.

The constable handed me the girl's identity card. Her photograph showed her with long blond hair and not the short black crop she now sported. Her name was Citizen Cora Maxwell. Age: 29. Height: 172 centimetres. Date of Arrival in Kaza-Blanka: 23 Brumaire, Year 82. Occupation: Artist.

It didn't take a detective to work out the situation.

Beautiful girl. Ugly man. What could bring them together in a shithole like this?

"So how much was he paying you? And what was he paying you for?"

The constable reacted like I'd slapped him. He did a funny twitch thing with his head then gave me a look that said, "Sir! You've gone too far."

Citizen Maxwell treated me to a cold, dead smile that amounted to an invitation for me to go roger myself. "Two hundred assignats, whoever you are. As to what that was in exchange for – that's between me and him."

"I'm Detective Inspector Seth Norton. There are two things you should know about me. One is that I'm bloody good at my job; the other is I'm a complete arsehole."

"I'd worked out *the other* for myself."

"It pays to advertise."

"So, Inspector Arsehole, ask your dumb questions, then fuck off."

I was starting to like her. "What happened here?"

"What do you think happened here?"

"We'll get through this bollocks a lot quicker if only one of us asks questions."

"If you don't mind me saying so, you look like a dirty old man."

She was referring to my beloved raincoat, which admittedly had seen better days, but had served me well throughout my policing career. I liked her a little less now. "I do mind you saying so. Now let's have your story before I lose patience and put you under arrest."

"Mostly it's the same story as every night. I was on Rue Dante looking for business. Some John picks me up and brings me back to this dump. We talk for a bit, then I suggest we hurry things along. *Sure, sure*, says the John. *But let's have a drink of sherry first.* So I force myself to neck a glass of Kaza Dry No. 2, which is something I intend to never do again. I've had cough medicine that tastes better.

"Anyway, the John takes off his clothes – all except his freaky underwear – and I think we're finally going to get down to business. Instead of which he asks me if I want to know his name, and I say *no I don't*. But he tells me anyway."

She paused, waiting for me to ask the obvious. There was clearly something of the drama queen in her.

"OK," I said. "I'll bite. What did he say his name was?"

"Jack the Revelator."

The hairs on my neck came to full attention. Drama queen or not, Cora Maxwell knew how to deliver a punch line. "You sure that's what he said?"

"Damn sure, Inspector."

"Then what happened?"

"I felt dizzy. I tried standing up and found myself flat on the floor. Then I passed out. Next thing I know, I'm on this bed with some flatfoot slapping my face and telling me to wake up."

"That was Constable Riley, sir," the uniform chipped in. "He was the first officer on the scene."

"The chap who's just parted ways with his breakfast?"

"That's him, sir. He's always doing that."

"But it wasn't him who found the body?"

"No, sir. That was Citizen Elmore Brecht from the Sanitation Department. He'd come to spray the apartment. When no one answered the door, he let himself in with a skeleton key. They're allowed to do that."

"What time was this?"

"About six."

"A bit bloody early, isn't it?"

"Not for an exterminator. Those guys work seriously long hours."

That figured. If my apartment was anything to go by, the cockroaches in Kaza were getting the upper hand. "Where is he now?"

"Spraying the rest of the building. I told him to wait till you got here but he said no can do. Too many cockroaches, not enough time. Do you want me to go fetch him?"

"No. Tell him to drop by the police station to make a statement. And warn him he's about to become famous." I pointed a finger at Cora Maxwell. "You're coming with me to the Precinct House."

"Am I under arrest?"

"Not if you co-operate."

I strode back into the living room. Sure enough, a bottle of Kaza Dry No. 2 sat on the table alongside a glass tumbler. "Bag those," I told Constable Riley, "and get them to the path lab, pronto."

Gene Hooke was packing away his equipment. "Did you get anything useful out of the girl?"

I turned to give Citizen Wyman a full-on view of the smug grin on my face. He was on his knees, examining the corpse. "You were wrong when you said this murder has nothing to do with the other six."

Wyman wiped his face with his handkerchief. "Oh? How come?"

Before I could answer, Studebaker strode out of the study looking pleased with himself. "You'll never believe what I found behind the books in the book case."

I took a punt. "A set of surgical instruments. The sort a maniac might use to remove organs from a corpse."

"Lucky guess."

"An educated one." I nodded in the direction of the

late Anton Delgado. "Sergeant Studebaker, meet the late, unlamented Jack the Revelator. Case closed."

---

2. Navigation

But, of course, it wasn't closed. Not by a long chalk. Although I was certain Delgado was Jack the Revelator, aka the West Side Ripper, I still had to prove it. I also had to account for how he ended up having the back of his head caved in with an iron poker.

That was the reason I was taking Cora Maxwell down to the Precinct House. She was going to tell me every little thing she'd seen and heard from the moment she'd first set eyes on Delgado right up to her wake-up call from Constable Riley. And she wasn't going to leave my sight until I was convinced there wasn't a gram of information left to be squeezed from her.

"You're one lucky lady," I told her as we headed for the nick in my slightly battered Kaza Sedan-7. "If things had gone the way Delgado had planned, it would be your body penciled in for a stay in the morgue, not his."

She took out a packet of Kaza Gold Filtered. "You mind if I smoke?"

I doubted it mattered whether I did or didn't. She was the sort of woman who generally got her own way, which was why she was in the front passenger seat when standard operating procedure said she should be in the back. I had by now ditched my original assessment of her as being some poor wee sparrow in desperate need of protection. She was more of a hawk.

"Knock yourself out." I turned up the air-con. "It's your lungs you're ruining."

With a wry smile, she popped her cigarette between her lips and lit it with a lighter she had tucked inside the fag packet. "How long have you been off them, Inspector?"

"What makes you think I was ever on them?"

"That sanctimonious crack about my lungs. And the way your face twitched when you saw the cigarettes. It's only a matter of time before you cave in, so enjoy your holier-than-thou kick while it lasts."

It was barely mid-morning but already the city was shimmering in the heat. Ragamuffin children chased sand devils beneath the gaze of old men sitting on canopied balconies smoking tobacco and qat.

"What a depressing neighbourhood." Citizen Maxwell expelled a tiny cloud of smoke with every syllable. "I detest brownstone."

"Tell me about it. I happen to live in one of these tenement blocks."

"Poor you."

Oh yes. Poor me. Still way down the waiting list for a decent pad despite being a Detective Inspector. You'd think my position would count for something, but apparently not.

"Being a cop," I'd been told by more than one Housing Department jerk, "doesn't entitle you to special treatment."

We passed a building site that had been a building site longer than I cared to remember. *BUILDING FOR A BETTER KAZA*, said a billboard. If the sign writer had been honest, he'd have added the word *SLOWLY*.

A handful of workmen lounged on the scaffolding, drinking vodka, playing cards and reading magazines. Perhaps sometime before they knocked off they would find it in them to lay a few bricks or mix some cement, but I wouldn't have put money on it.

A left turn took us onto the Strip where traffic was building up nicely. Brightly coloured tuk-tuks, rickshaws, buses and taxis jostled one another like a carnival of exotic animals. I loved the cacophony of it all – the jungle cries of engines, horns and bells punctuated with angry expletives. For me, the Strip was what Kaza was all about. I owed my sanity to the nights I'd spent cruising its bars, jazz clubs and clip joints.

By day, the Strip wore a mask of respectability. Its coffee shops, wine bars and sidewalk cafes were the very model of gentility and charm. Between dawn and dusk, this was where the fashionista and intelligentsia gathered to swap fashion tips, outrageous gossip and the odd gem of philosophical wisdom.

We stopped at a red light not a dozen steps from the Cafe Voltaire. When I saw a sign saying the place was under new ownership and closed for refurbishment, a little piece of me died.

Citizen Maxwell followed the direction of my scowl. "A dive," she said. "They should dynamite the joint."

And that's when it came to me. A memory of a night in the Cafe Voltaire, surrounded by goonies and gawpers and people who thought they were being cool when all they were doing was disappearing up their own jacksies.

Calling itself *The Home of Performance Art,* the Cafe Voltaire prided itself on hosting the edgiest shows in town. And by *edgiest* they clearly meant *most pretentious*.

I recalled some guy on stage cutting up the clothes he was wearing until he was completely naked. And that was followed by a man creating spontaneous poetry by reading out every sixth word of a pornographic novel.

I shouldn't like shit like that, but I do.

It must have been two in the morning when Cora Maxwell took to the stage. Only she didn't call herself Cora Maxwell; she was *The Silence*.

The joint was almost empty. When I'd walked in with my two buddies, we'd had problems finding a table. Now my buddies were gone and I had a table all to myself and could have had several more if I'd wanted.

There wasn't enough cigarette smoke in the air for my taste, so I lit a Kaza No. 6 and watched a couple of stagehands wheel what looked like a random assemblage of junk onto the stage.

Here we go again, I thought. *Yet more found art. And now I get to endure some self-deluded geek telling me how a trip to the municipal garbage dump transformed their understanding of the boundaries of art.*

A spotlight kicked in, giving me a clearer view of the whatever-the-hell-it-was. Now it resembled a control console, not unlike the one the traffic department used for controlling Kaza's traffic lights.

Standing up, I was able to make out a keyboard that might have been cannibalised from an electric organ. Sitting down again, I took a swig of whiskey and braced myself for a riot of tedious nonsense.

"Ladies and gentlemen," said the M.C. from the side of the stage, "I give you the Silence!"

A smattering of applause. One lone snigger. And a wall of indifference.

She had on an elegant black dress, the sort people wear to the opera. It was offset by a purple sash and a pearl necklace. Her hair was the way it was in her identity card photo – golden and shoulder length.

Sitting behind the console on a piano stool, she peeled off her long black gloves then set about bringing the machine to life by flicking switches and hitting buttons.

The contraption hummed. Electrical valves glowed. Relays engaged. Lights flickered.

With a chattering like joke shop wind-up teeth, the machine chomped away at a strip of computer tape wrapped around a metal spool. When the last of the tape had disappeared into the machine's innards, the woman who called herself *The Silence* spoke into a microphone. "Ladies and gentlemen, it never snows in Kaza-Blanka. We may all have experienced snow in our past lives, but we have no way of knowing. Some believe snow doesn't actually exist, and who can blame them? We live in a city surrounded by desert. Heatstroke awaits anyone who ventures out during the day without a hat or a parasol. We could not survive here without air conditioning, so it's hard to imagine anywhere so cold that rain becomes solid." She raised her hands and closed her eyes. "One day, I hope to know how it feels to have snow fall on my skin. The music I'm about to play is inspired by that hope. It's called *Midnight Snow*."

Her fingers descended onto the keyboard and brought forth a Dm7 chord that rose like a fountain and dissipated into a fine mist of tumbling notes. Its tonality was electronic and ethereal, mechanical and magical.

The piece that followed was a requiem and a lullaby rolled into one. It was about life; it was about death. Unhurried, mournful and majestic, it stayed with me for days afterward.

The Silence didn't seem to play the music so much as distil its essence from the air. By flicking switches and tuning dials, she was able to change the voice of her machine. Sometimes it sounded like a solitary violin or trumpet, other times a whole orchestra.

When she was done, I was drained.

"What was that thing you played?" I asked Citizen Maxwell as the lights turned green and the traffic on the Strip got flowing again. "That machine of yours?"

"I call it an electro-clavier."

"I'd sure like to meet the geek who put that together. He must be some sort of genius."

"Actually, Inspector Arsehole, I built it myself. And me a mere woman! Who'd have thought?"

That was my foot well and truly in it. And just when we were beginning to get along. "You played it beautifully," I said, desperate to remedy the situation. "And you have a real gift for composition."

"Thank you," she said acidly. "Coming from you, that means so much."

---

3. Interrogation

The interrogation did not go according to plan – the plan being to sweat Citizen Maxwell in a cell for a couple of hours before hauling her arse into an interrogation room and hitting her with the good cop/bad cop routine. My ungentlemanly intentions unraveled the moment we stepped into the reception area and someone wolf whistled.

"Knock it off, Radcliffe," I warned. "This one ain't for you."

Radcliffe licked her lips then mouthed a kiss at Citizen Maxwell. "I bet you look real sweet in handcuffs, honey."

Sniggers all round.

"Not half as sweet as I do in leg restraints," Citizen Maxwell retorted. "I'll send you some photos if you like."

More sniggers. Radcliffe was baffled.

Sergeant Melrose manned the desk. Handsome, polite, well-read, he was everything a desk sergeant shouldn't be.

"Why are you still here, Constable?" he asked. "Shouldn't you be on traffic duty?"

Radcliffe's face took on a rosy complexion. Traffic duty was for rookies and those who fucked up. She was no rookie. "I'm on my way."

As she walked by, she gave Citizen Maxwell's backside a slap. Citizen Maxwell blew her a kiss.

I turned my gaze on the other uniforms hanging around gawping.

"Fuck off the lot of you. Anyone still here in five seconds is joining Radcliffe on traffic duty."

Four seconds later and the only people in the reception area were Citizen Maxwell, myself and Sergeant Melrose.

I guided Citizen Maxwell to the desk.

"I do so apologise for the behaviour of my colleagues," said Sergeant Melrose. "I hope you weren't offended."

"Boys will be boys."

"And morons will be morons."

"Citizen Maxwell," I announced, "is a material witness to a homicide. She is here of her own volition and has volunteered to make a statement."

"You're not booking her?" Melrose seemed relieved. "I presume you want Interview Room 3?"

Oh yes. Interview Room 3, a.k.a. the fish tank – so called because of the two-way mirror which made it a magnet for the type of cop who gets their jollies watching beautiful women being put through the grinder.

"I'll take Citizen Maxwell's statement in my office. Make sure we're not disturbed."

My office had started life as a store room, which explained the lack of windows and the ghostly outlines of departed filing cabinets on the floor. Not that you could see much of the floor on account of the cardboard boxes housing the best part of my record collection.

Not only did I love my office, I loved that I loved it. When I'd made D.I., the Chief had allocated me the place as his way of saying the promotion wasn't his idea. He wanted me to hate the place, so I made damn sure I didn't.

"Nice," said Citizen Maxwell as I scrambled over the desk to get to my chair. "So compact too."

I presumed she was talking about the room.

"You'll have to forgive the mess," I told her. "I keep most of my more valuable belongings here. That way they're less likely to get eaten."

"Eaten?"

"The rats in my apartment block have developed a taste for vinyl."

She pulled a 78 out of one of the boxes. "Art Mankey? A bit old school for my tastes."

"His later stuff sucks big time," I conceded. "It's only his first dozen or so discs that interest me. They show a lot of promise that was never realised."

Citizen Maxwell put the disc back where she found it. "Are all your records 78s?"

"33s are an abomination."

"I agree. The sound quality leaves a lot to be desired."

"And don't get me started on stereo."

"OK. I won't." Citizen Maxwell sat down and made herself as comfortable as circumstances allowed.

I recorded her statement on a reel-to-reel tape recorder. With a little prompting from me here and there, she told much the same story she'd given back at Anton Delgado's apartment.

When she got to the part about Delgado announcing he was Jack the Revelator, I jumped in. "Do you recall his exact words?"

"*I am Jack the Revelator, instrument of God's will.*"

"Had you heard the name before?"

"No. But you obviously had. When I said it, you went pale – not that your face is overly blessed with colour in the first place. Do you want to tell me what this is all about, Inspector?"

"Finish up, then I'll give you the full skinny."

She completed her testimony in a few more sentences and I hit the tape recorder's off switch.

"Whisky?" I retrieved my work bottle from under the desk.

"I'm not sure I should. Whatever your friend Jack slipped me has left me with a hangover."

"What you need is a hair of the dog." I retrieved two glasses and poured. "This will flush the drug out of your system – I think."

"And I'm going to need a drink to steady my nerves, because you're just about to tell me what a nasty man Jack the Revelator is and I'm going to be all a-tremble."

"Spot on. Now drink."

Citizen Maxwell did as she was told. I half-expected her to crease up, clutching her belly and yelling, "It burns! It burns!" She didn't even pull a face.

"A seasoned whisky drinker," I observed. "Cheers!"

I hoped she didn't notice my hand shaking as I lifted the glass to my lips.

"Well go on," Citizen Maxwell challenged. "Now that we're both fortified, let me have it."

"You've heard of the West Side Ripper?"

"I recognised you as the copper who's hunting him. Remember?"

"Oh yeah. Well, you've no doubt read in the papers all the gory details about him cutting open his victims and making off with their internal organs. It kind of gives the impression that the press know as much about the Ripper as we do."

"And you're going to tell me they don't."

"Well, there's one detail we managed to keep from the gentlemen of the Fourth Estate. Once it became public knowledge that I was on the case, the Ripper took to sending me letters. *Dear Pen Pal* is the way they always began. Then there'd be a few pages of what I can only describe as the writings of a lunatic. Stuff about him being the instrument of God's will sent to Kaza-Blanka to punish the unworthy and so forth. After that, he tended to get personal. According to him, I was the lousiest copper in history with absolutely zero chance of catching him. It was the sort of crap you'd expect from a deluded psycho. Anyway, the point is he always signed off as – you've guessed it – Jack the Revelator."

"So, thanks to me, you now have a serial killer in your morgue. I seem to have done your job for you."

"Don't flatter yourself. All you did was get yourself knocked out. That hardly falls under the heading of sterling police work. Another few days and I'd have nabbed the bastard good and proper."

"Oh dear. I seem to have rattled your cage and that wasn't my intention. I do apologise, Inspector. The nick was entirely yours and I'm no more than an innocent bystander."

"Unlike the mystery man who saved your life by doing away with Anton Delgado, aka the West Side Ripper, aka Jack the Revelator." A slug of whisky soothed my ruffled feathers. I topped up Citizen Maxwell's glass to show there were no hard feelings. "Unfortunately, by doing so, he's replaced one set of mysteries with another. I don't suppose you've any clue as to who he might be?"

"I'm afraid my powers of observation aren't at their best when I'm unconscious."

"You didn't notice anyone following you to Delgado's flat?"

"Nope."

"Or anyone hanging around outside? Or maybe you saw someone odd on the Rue Dante?"

"It's the Rue Dante. Of course I saw someone odd." Citizen Maxwell took out her cigarettes and waved the pack in my direction. I shook my head and made a gesture to convey she was quite welcome to fill my office with noxious fumes. "Of course, there's one obvious question that would be bugging me if I were in your position."

"And what's that?"

"What was a poker doing in an apartment with no fireplace?"

Before I could even begin to think of a good answer, the phone rang and I snatched it up. "Norton."

"You and your big mouth, Norton!" It was the Chief. "What do you mean by flapping your gums at the press?"

"With all due respect, Chief, I don't know what you're talking about."

"Then I suppose you can't explain why I've just had some dipshit from the *Kaza Telegraph* telling me we've caught the West Side Ripper?"

"I swear to you Chief, I've not spoken to the press and I've told no one at the station that this homicide has anything to do with the Ripper."

"If you're lying, Norton, I'm going to arrange for you to spend quality time with some of the villains you've banged up. Do I make myself clear?"

"As always, Chief."

"I've had to call a press conference to make sure the press tell the story we want them to tell. And you know how much I hate press conferences."

About as much as a wasp hates jam.

"Do you want me to be there, Chief?"

"So you can hog all the credit for a team effort? Not on your Nelly." Which was the Chief's way of saying if anyone was going to be hogging all the credit it was him. "There's an inbound flight due to land at midday. According to the passenger list, there's a certain Clayton Astley aboard. You remember the little shit-weasel, don't you?"

"Sure, Chief." How could I forget? Before fleeing Kaza, Astley had been an underworld enforcer, inflicting pain and injury on anyone who dared displease his clients. If he'd stuck around just a day longer, I would have had him under lock and key and heading for the penitentiary where he belonged. But someone had tipped him the wink and he'd beaten me to the airport by a matter of minutes. Once he was airside that was that. I couldn't touch him.

But now he was back and I could tie up one of the biggest loose ends of my career. So far, today was turning out a lot better than I'd expected.

"Get your butt down to the airport, Norton," the Chief growled. "And see he doesn't get away again."

---

4. Incarceration

Kaza Airport. One landing strip. One terminal building. And an electrified fence patrolled by fierce bastards with fierce dogs.

Having the Arrivals Lounge to myself, I sat by the observation window from where I enjoyed a clear view of the landing strip and the desert beyond. In the distance, the Kaza Mountains were a grey smudge on the horizon.

The clock on the wall told me it was 9:90 – 10 minutes before the flight was due. Which gave me time to think about Anton Delgado and his timely demise.

Citizen Maxwell's remark about the poker stuck in my mind. Not only was there no fireplace in the apartment, there was no poker rest or any other fireside paraphernalia, which suggested that the poker had been introduced to the crime scene by the killer, which in turn suggested premeditation.

There'd been no sign of a break in and the front

door was the sort that locked automatically once closed. It looked likely that Delgado had not only known his murderer but had trusted him enough to let him into his flat in the middle of the night. And that despite the fact that he had an unconscious woman in his bedroom lined up to be his next victim.

So why had someone come calling on Jack the Revelator at such an ungodly hour, and why had Jack not sent him on his way?

There was one other thing that bothered me. Jack had his back to the killer when the killer struck. You'd think under the circumstances he would be more on his guard. It was yet another indicator that killer and victim were close.

Everything pointed to the worst possible conclusion and I tried to find a flaw in my reasoning but couldn't. Until I had more information, I was going to have to live with the likelihood that Jack had an accomplice and the killings would continue.

The distant drone of a twin-engined turbo-prop brought me back to the here and now. Looking up, I could see the aircraft on the horizon.

A voice leapt out of the public address system. "Flight 001 from Elsewhere is now approaching the airport. All immigration staff to their stations, please. Passengers waiting to board the outbound Flight 002 to Elsewhere are asked to remain in the Departures Lounge until given further instructions. Thank you."

From a hitherto locked door, a platoon of airport staff trooped into the Arrivals Lounge. Some wore the blue and white uniform of the Immigration Service but most were in civvies. A couple of guys sporting Red Cross arm bands flanked a uniformed nurse who, despite having her hair in a bun and wearing no discernible make-up, looked rather tasty.

"Detective Inspector Norton! Long time no see!" Jules Wilde was suddenly upon me, shaking my hand

and slapping me on the shoulder. "How have you been keeping?"

"Fine. How's tricks in the Immigration Department?"

"Never mind that! What about you catching the West Side Ripper? I bet that sourpuss Chief of yours was pleased!"

Ever since we'd spent a rowdy night on the Strip, getting pissed and creeping into joints two fine upstanding citizens like ourselves shouldn't even know existed, Jules had decided that I was – as he'd once drunkenly expressed it -- his "bestest buddy in the whole wide world".

Jules probably had dozens of "bestest buddies in the whole wide world"; he was that kind of a guy. He seemed to take an instant liking to everyone he met, and they to him.

"I hear you got promoted," I said in an attempt to deflect the conversation.

"Deputy Head of Resettlement and Integration."

"It's been a long time coming, Jules. I'm pleased for you."

"Yeah, yeah, yeah. But what about the Ripper? Rumour has it that he's someone high up in City Hall. Perhaps even the Mayor."

"Now you're fishing."

"You bet."

"Well I ain't biting."

Jules looked at his clipboard. "I see you've come to arrest that slime ball Astley. You've got to wonder how bad life in Elsewhere must be when the likes of him get desperate enough to return here to face prison."

"99% of people who leave Kaza don't come back," I pointed out. "So I guess they must be happy wherever they are. Or at least happier."

"Do you ever think about it, Inspector? Returning to Elsewhere?"

"Not really. A man knows when he's where he belongs."

"I reckon before I arrived I was a cop like you. Sometimes I wake up and find myself thinking I must get down to the Precinct House to crack the case. They say some of our dreams are actually memories of Elsewhere. Do you suppose it's true?"

"Perhaps." I had to raise my voice because the plane was directly over us as it turned towards the runway. "But how would we know which dreams are memories and which are just dreams?"

"I never remember my dreams anyway."

Jules broke away to take up position by the entrance. A sign above the door cautioned that anyone leaving the lounge to go airside would be forcibly deported to Elsewhere. No *ifs*. No *buts*. No right of appeal.

There was another much larger sign on the wall. In white lettering on a red background, it presented the reader with the first chapter of the so-called Citizens Charter.

ATTENTION NEWCOMERS.

You have come to Kaza-Blanka of your own free will in order to leave your past behind. You remember nothing of that past because you consented to the erasure of your memories of where you were and what you did before boarding the plane to Kaza-Blanka. If you have been in Kaza-Blanka before, your memories of here remain intact, although it may take time for them to return in full. Your memories of the place you must now call Elsewhere will be given back to you should you ever opt to return to your old life.

This is a new beginning for you.

What you did in Elsewhere is no longer relevant. Whatever drove you here cannot follow you. Your crimes need not haunt you. Your sins are forgiven. Your troubles are no more. The past is erased.

The Twin City of Kaza-Blanka welcomes you without reservation or prejudice.

Here we believe in government of the people, by the people, for the people. We also believe that each should take according to their needs and give according to their ability. If you share these values, then you will surely thrive.

Liberty, Equality and Fraternity for all!

The plane touched down and taxied up to the terminal. With a final burst of splutters, the engines shut down and the propellers came to rest.

I unbuttoned my raincoat to ensure my holstered gun was on view. Then I took out my handcuffs and Clayton Astley's arrest warrant.

The staircase tender trundled up to the plane. When it was in place, the passenger door slid open and the passengers began to disembark. As usual, most of them looked as if they couldn't quite believe the enormous step they'd taken. Just about every last one of them would be wondering if they'd done the right thing or made the biggest mistake of their life. Of course, with no memory of anything they did before boarding Flight 001, they had no way of knowing.

The p.a. burst into life again. "Passengers are reminded that they must go straight to the Arrivals Lounge. Anyone still airside when the door closes will be deported back to Elsewhere."

The immigrants carried identical brown suitcases. This, along with whatever money they'd transferred to the Bank of Kaza, would form the embryo of their new lives in Kaza-Blanka.

Clayton Astley was the last to leave the plane.

Understandably in no hurry to fall into my welcoming arms, he kept looking over his shoulder at the plane.

As he reached the door, he clocked me and the wind in his sails failed him. He stood stock still and I have never seen a face filled with so much uncertainty in all my life.

"Do come in, Citizen Astley," Jules Wilde taunted. "We don't want you getting sunstroke, do we?"

Astley didn't seem to hear. He stared at me like I was some awful apparition. Perhaps he was hoping to make me disappear through the power of wishful thinking.

"The terminal door will close in twenty-five seconds," the p.a. warned. "Anyone still airside when the door closes will be transported back to Elsewhere. Please make your way indoors now."

The other passengers were being escorted out to the esplanade where a bus awaited them. After a briefing from Jules or one of his minions, they would be taken to their new homes, given their social security numbers and told what job had been allocated to them.

Astley was like a frightened animal. I sensed that any sudden move on my part would cause him to scurry back to the plane, leaving me with no prisoner and the certainty of yet another bollocking from the Chief.

Jules looked at the clock. "You have ten seconds, Citizen Astley. Nine... eight... seven... six... five..."

With a scowl, Astley stepped through the door. It swung shut behind him and locked itself with a click that must have sounded to the poor sap like the hammer of a gun being pulled back.

"Welcome to Kaza-Blanka, Citizen Astley." Jules clicked his heels and saluted. "Your escort awaits."

I strolled up to the little skid mark and gave him my best smile so he could be in no doubt how pleased I was to see him. "Do me a favour, Astley. Punch me in the face and make a run for it. I think you'd look good with a bullet in your back."

Astley let go of his suitcase and proffered his hands for cuffing. "Still the same arsehole as ever you were, Inspector. Things in Kaza-Blanka never really change, do they?"

Back at the nick, I was disappointed to find Citizen Maxwell gone. Of course she had every right to leave whenever she wanted, but I was miffed that she hadn't at least left a note to say goodbye.

I spent the next few hours wading through largely pointless paperwork with a break to watch the Chief's press conference on the television in the squad room. As expected, I barely got a mention, and the way the Chief told it, you'd think he'd personally busted open the case with a combination of dogged determination and great personal sacrifice.

The one good mark he earned from me was for saying nothing about Citizen Maxwell. In the Chief's version of events, the West Side Ripper had been found dead in his apartment by an unidentified member of the public. Suicide, the Chief said without actually saying it, was the likeliest scenario.

"Why," asked a lady reporter from the *Kaza Star*, "would he have killed himself?"

"Nobody said he killed himself. But to me it looks like he knew I was closing in on him so took the coward's way out."

Bleugh! It took three slugs of whisky to rid my mouth of the bad taste left by the Chief's performance.

Paperwork done, I decided to knock off early. I reckoned I deserved it.

5. Libation

Samson's Bar on the Strip was my idea of what a bar should be – all wood and dinginess. What little daylight managed to get in fell through a grimy skylight to be sliced up by wooden beams so it hit the floor in stripes. Everything in the place that wasn't black and white seemed to be brown – the exception being the walls. They sported a shade of yellow I've seen nowhere else.

As I parked my arse on a stool at the bar, Jimmy the Goose already had a shot lined up for me. I downed it in one.

"Been that kind of a day, has it?" Jimmy topped up my glass. "I saw your boss on the television blowing his horn. You weren't kidding when you said he's a totally up himself."

"He'll get his," I declared with no certainty that he would. "But bollocks to him. I'm here to celebrate. Will you do me a steak sandwich, Jimmy?"

"You want it at your usual table?"

"Where else?"

My usual table was occupied, but not for long. One jerk of Jimmy's thumb was enough to send the interlopers scurrying off elsewhere.

Jimmy left me with a beer, a bottle of Kaza No. 5 and a bowl of peanuts. I sat watching television, knowing I was being watched in turn. The denizens of Samson's Bar were aware I was a cop and had something to do with the West Side Ripper. They wanted nothing more than for me to shoot my mouth off and give them inside info they could impress their friends with. But that wasn't going to happen and they knew it.

The telly was tuned to Kaza News 10. It was all sports peppered with commercial breaks and pointless weather forecasts. Today was sunny. Tomorrow would be sunny too. And there'd be no break in the sunshine until the rainy season arrived.

I was halfway through my steak sandwich when an item about some piss-poor basketball team was interrupted by what the newsreader called a *breaking story*.

"We're now going over to the Sanitation Department where Kaza News 10 reporter Citizen Ed Crowe has just caught up with the man who tracked down and killed the so-called West Side Ripper."

The picture cut to a head and shoulders of Ed Crowe. "Thank you, Bill. I'm standing on the steps leading to the entrance to the Sanitation Department with Sanitation Engineer Citizen Elmore Brecht, a brave man with an extraordinary story to tell."

There was a cut to a two shot. Elmore Brecht stood on the steps in his work overalls, his canister of cockroach poison at his side.

"Citizen Brecht, could you tell us in your own words how you cracked a case that has baffled the Kaza Police Department from the very get-go?"

As Crowe pointed a microphone at him, Elmore Brecht grinned the cheesiest of grins made all the cheesier by the presence of a gold molar. "Well, Ed, it was like this, see. I was on duty in the Rue Morgue, up nice and early so I could kill me some cockroaches while most folks was still in bed. My canister of roach powder was empty, so I went back to my van to refill it. As I was doing so, I saw this car pull up and I knew there was something bad about it. Don't ask how I knew; I just did.

"Anyways, this dude gets out and he is the meanest, most evil-looking dude I ever did see. *Elmore*, I says to myself, *there something ain't right about this*. So I hide behind my van and watch what the dude gets up to."

"And what did he get up to?"

"I'm just coming to that, Ed. What he got up to is a

whole load of no good. I saw him open the trunk of his car and take out what I thought must be a dog he'd run over or something but which I soon realised was a woman. I didn't know if she was dead or just plain drunk, but I knew something was up 'cause no one brings their date home in the trunk of a car no matter how juiced they are.

"So anyways, I follow the dude at a safe distance into an apartment block and up one – no, two – flights of stairs to what I now know was his apartment. Now, I ain't never peeped through no keyholes before, but this looked like a good time to start. So I get down on my knees and I peep and can hardly believe what I'm seeing. The girl's awake and standing butt-naked right in the middle of the living room. I could tell she was drugged because she had this glazed look like people get when they inhale roach powder. I knew she was there in body but her mind was someplace else." Elmore's grin grew cheesier. "May I take a moment, Ed, to tell that young lady that she has one hell of a fine body, and if she's ever at a loose end for something to do, she can contact me through the Sanitation Department. Man, that is one great pair of jubbers she's got."

A panicked Ed Crowe attempted a laugh which sounded like a cat being strangled. "I'm sure the lady's got the message, Elmore. In the meantime, our viewers are dying to know what happened next."

"Oh yeah. Well then the dude starts saying some crazy stuff about how all women are whores and they should be ashamed of themselves and he's going to teach them all a lesson. And then he produces this real nasty looking knife – about this long and real, real sharp – and I just know I gotta do something.

"So I break down the door and, without a moment's thought for my own safety, I throw myself at the dude and we have quite a wrestling match. And all the time he's trying to stab me with his knife but I don't let him 'cause I've been stabbed before and know how much it hurts. Then eventually I hit him on the back of the head with a poker and kill him."

"A poker?"

"Yeah. I carry one with me most times. It's handy for getting at roaches in awkward places."

From behind the bar, Jimmy gave vent to a dirty guffaw. "Is that how it happened, Inspector? Have we all been saved from certain death by a bug exterminator?"

"The guy is full of shit," I said, loud enough for everyone to hear. "The Ripper was already dead when Brecht found him."

"So, if he didn't kill the West Side Ripper, who did?"

"I only wish I knew." My appetite for food was gone. I pushed away what was left of my sandwich and threw whisky down my throat.

If she's ever at a loose end for something to do, she can contact me...

In your dreams, Citizen Brecht. Jubbers indeed!

I didn't want to be in Samson's any more. All the things that usually made it great – the dinginess, the grubbiness, the general air of sleaze – now served to depress me. It was as if Elmore Brecht's disgusting essence had somehow seeped out of the television screen.

I had the blues and this wasn't the place to drink them away.

As I reached for my wallet, something happened to change my mind. Cora Maxwell walked in.

Now she was out of hooker mode and dressed like a jazz cat in black slacks, white T shirt, black satin jacket and white fedora, she seemed a whole different woman. She looked stunning and a couple of wolf whistles said I wasn't the only one who thought so.

"All right, you guys. Knock it on the head." Jimmy

whacked the top of his bar with a pool cue. "Just remember your manners."

Citizen Maxwell took off her sunglasses. "Thank you, Jimmy. It's good to know there are still some gentlemen left in this city."

"Your usual table, Citizen Maxwell?"

"I'm rather hoping the Inspector will invite me to join him for a drink."

If ever there was a moment when Jimmy the Goose could have been knocked down with a feather, this was surely it. As he escorted Citizen Maxwell to my table, he gave me a look that was a curious mixture of respect and puzzlement.

I decided to play it casual. "So you two know each other?"

"The lady is a regular here," said Jimmy. "Only this is the first time I've seen her all dolled up like this."

Citizen Maxwell sat down. "My usual, please, Jimmy."

The barman trotted off like a dog sent to fetch his mistress's slippers. All his hard edges seemed to have dissolved away.

"A regular?" I echoed. "Here?"

"I pop in every now and then."

"How come I've never seen you?"

"You have. You've just never noticed."

"Don't think I'm trying to flatter you, Citizen Maxwell, but you are not the sort of woman I would fail to notice."

"When the fancy takes me, I can be the sort of woman no man notices. Why do you think I call myself the Silence?"

"There's a difference between silence and invisibility."

"Not if you're blind, Inspector."

She had a point. Or I thought she did. Frankly, I didn't know if she was being profound or just plain pretentious. She was playing mind games with me and had the advantage of first serve.

"You always come in here alone, Inspector, like this is your special place and you don't want to share it."

"I'm sharing it now, aren't I?"

"I can go away if you like."

"Don't you dare."

Citizen Maxwell took a sip of my whisky. "Jimmy's still watering it down, I see. It's a wonder you don't arrest him."

"If the police arrested every bar owner in the city who adulterated their liquor, there'd be no room in the Penitentiary for anyone else."

Jimmy the Goose plonked a tall glass on the table. "There you go, Citizen Maxwell. One gin and tonic on the house."

"Thank you, Jimmy. I sure appreciate it."

Jimmy hovered, as if waiting to be dismissed. I had never seen him do it before and it made me nervous.

"Hey!" he said, suddenly, slapping my arm with the back of his hand. "Tell Citizen Maxwell about the kook on the telly. The one who says he killed the West Side Ripper."

Damn Jimmy. I could have done without him bringing that up.

"I'm sure Citizen Maxwell doesn't want to know about kooks on the telly," I said, attempting to express with the inflection of my voice that Jimmy had outstayed his welcome.

But Jimmy wasn't one for taking hints. "*Jubbers!* That's what he said. You ever hear that expression before? I run a bar and I could have sworn I'd heard every possibly term for a lady's – and I hope you'll pardon the expression, Citizen Maxwell – tits but I gotta say jubbers is a new one on me."

Imagine tin foil coming into contact with your fillings at the very instant someone runs their fingernails down a blackboard and you realise you're only wearing a vest and you're standing in the middle of a crowded shop and someone takes a photo. Imagine that feeling and multiply it by a million. Now you're somewhere in the vicinity of where I was.

"Jubbers?" Citizen Maxwell seemed to chew over the word in her mind. The slow lifting of an eyebrow showed she was processing it. "You say he killed the West Side Ripper?"

"No," Jimmy corrected. "That's what *he* says. The inspector says he's full of crap and I believe him."

"And he said jubbers in relation to what?"

"The girl the Ripper was about to turn into a pyjama case when he burst in and heroically saved her."

"Sounds like a brave man."

"Except he ain't. He made the whole thing up and in doing so has robbed the inspector of his fully-deserved glory. Right, Inspector?"

The conversation was taking me in no direction I wanted to go, but the current was too strong to swim against. "As it happens, the Ripper was already dead when Elmore Brecht found him."

"And the broad?"

"Unconscious."

"Did she have nice jubbers like the guy said?"

"A nice everything, Jimmy. The girl was pure class."

"And unconscious, you say?" For a moment, Jimmy was lost in some sordid reverie before his inner decency pulled him back. "She wasn't hurt, was she? Or injured in any way?"

"As far as I can tell, she came out of it just fine."

"Good. I hate it when broads get hurt. It ain't right."

The arrival of a fresh customer left Jimmy with no choice but to drift back to the bar. I sat staring up at the skylight, wondering if I'd set a new record for embarrassment.

Citizen Maxwell touched my hand. "So I have nice jubbers?"

"Elmore Brecht's words – not mine."

"That's right. You said I had a nice everything."

"If you care to look beneath my raincoat, you'll find my gun in its holster. You have my full permission to take it out and shoot me."

She laughed. "Oh you poor man. You're not used to complimenting women, are you?"

"That was a compliment?"

"Yes it was, Inspector Arsehole. Now order me another drink and let's discuss our plans for the evening."

---

6. Relaxation

We took in a movie. *Dark Encounter* with Howard Taylor and Naomi Thurman. Two people arrive in Kaza-Blanka on Flight 001 from Elsewhere. He sets up shop as a dentist; she makes jewellery and sells it from a stall in Penny Lane Market. They fall in love but never consummate their passion.

And why do they deny themselves the intimacy they so clearly crave? Because they're both certain they've left someone behind in Elsewhere. Someone they loved. Someone they cared for. Someone they remember absolutely nothing about.

They couldn't let go and they didn't know what it was that they couldn't let go of. Or something like that.

To be honest, I didn't get it.

As night fell and the city became noticeably cooler in both temperature and temperament, Citizen Maxwell and I strolled along the Embankment and talked about *Dark Encounter*. Or, rather, she talked, I listened.

"The way I see it," she said, "neither character had left behind anything or anybody worth a damn, but they couldn't bring themselves to admit it. They were unable to accept that their lives really were empty and meaningless.

"For them, as it is with most of us poor lost souls in Kaza, Elsewhere was a blank screen onto which they could project their hopes and dreams. It was that *other place* where all things are possible and the virtuous are rewarded for their goodness. Remember what the Naomi Thurman character said towards the end of the film? That thing about why wait for death when we can have the afterlife right now?"

"*Just hop on a plane,*" I quoted, "*and all our troubles will be behind us.*"

Citizen Maxwell proceeded to dissect the film scene by scene, beat by beat. From the allusions and comparisons she made, she was clearly a real film buff and had probably seen every film ever released in Kaza at least once.

So deep, I thought with admiration. *For a prostitute.*

We came to the Bridge of Sighs and stood between the two bronze statues – one a lion, the other a unicorn – that guarded its entrance. Ahead of us, gargoyles crouched along either side of the bridge like a grotesque guard of honour.

"It's magnificent," said Cora. "The unknown artisans who carved these beasts were true craftsmen."

"It gives me the creeps," I admitted. "But you're right. It *is* magnificent."

We climbed onto the observation platform. Across the Kaza River, the city of Blanka with its white towers, domes and minarets stood as still and enigmatic as ever.

The large sign that warned people not to cross the

bridge and not to stop others from doing so must have been recently repainted. It was defaced with far less graffiti than the last time I'd seen it.

Citizen Maxwell lit a cigarette. "It's a strange law that forbids people to prevent others from harming themselves. If I was running the city, I'd make the Bridge of Sighs impassable."

It was a sentiment often expressed and seldom argued with. Like many laws governing Kaza-Blanka, nobody understood why this one had been enacted, when it had been enacted or even who it had been enacted by. But it was the law and there were penalties for breaking it.

"Have you ever felt an urge to cross the Bridge of Sighs?" Citizen Maxwell asked.

"No. I've seen what happens to people who do. It isn't pleasant."

"You've only seen the ones who come back. What about the ones who don't?"

"They all come back."

"Maybe some don't. People go missing from Kaza all the time. Perhaps some are made welcome in the White City."

"Who by?" I felt a surge of irritation. "Look at the place. The buildings are empty. It's more like a mausoleum than a city."

"So how do people get back from there when they've had their memories erased?"

"They return over the Bridge of Sighs." I'd seen them with my own eyes, walking like zombies with blank expressions and no idea of anything at all. Thankfully, they always returned at night when there was a curfew around the Bridge and no one to see them except a small team from the Department of Immigration specially trained to deal with what were effectively walking vegetables.

"What I mean is," Citizen Maxwell persisted, like a

schoolboy picking at a scab that wouldn't come away, "how do they get back to the Bridge of Sighs? Someone must guide them there, otherwise they'd be wandering around Blanka until they died of hunger or thirst."

"Nobody guides them. It's just instinct."

"You seem quite agitated all of a sudden, Inspector. I hope it's not something I said."

"No," I lied. "I guess I'm one of those people who like to pretend Blanka doesn't exist."

"That puts you in the majority." Citizen Maxwell drew on her cigarette and allowed blue smoke to drift out of her mouth and merge with the evening breeze. "I go one better than those who pretend the place doesn't exist."

"Oh? How?"

"I truly believe that it doesn't." Citizen Maxwell got to her feet and put her cigarette out on the warning board. "You need a drink, Inspector."

She was right. "I know a great little bar not ten minutes from here. You'll like it."

"We could go there. Or we could hop on a tram and head back to my place. I think I have enough whisky to keep you going till breakfast."

---

7. Fornication

We hopped off the tram at the Place de la Concorde and took our lives in our hands crossing all six lanes of the busiest road in Kaza with seemingly every tuk-tuk driver and moped rider in Kaza intent on mowing us down.

It was only when we were back on a pavement and the imminent threat of death was removed that I realised we were headed for the Artists' Colony. I knew already that Citizen Maxwell lived on the Rue Matisse but I hadn't until now given any thought as to where in

Kaza that might be. Somehow I'd pictured her living in some squalid little shit hole or conversely a luxury penthouse. It seemed to me that prostitutes were always housed in one or the other.

The colony was surrounded by a high wall upon which cameras perched like monocular crows. A barrier across the only road into the colony served to help keep out the hoi polloi.

In the gatehouse, an armed guard sat watching television. Seeing Citizen Maxwell, his face lost its bored expression. "Evening, Citizen Maxwell," he chimed, opening the door to let us in.

"Evening, Sam. How's the wife?"

"A lot better now. She thanks you for the flowers." Sam looked me up and down. "You're a cop. I used to be one myself until I took a bullet in the hip."

"I'm sorry to hear that."

"Sorry to hear what? That I was a cop or that I took a bullet?"

"Both, I guess."

"I ain't sorry about neither. I've got me a nice pension, I meet lots of famous people and I get to watch television at work. Kind of a cushy set-up, wouldn't you say, Citizen?"

"Apart from the television bit. There's never anything worth watching."

"You've got to lower your standards, is all. Makes life easier."

"Quite the philosopher, aren't we?"

"And one heck of a television critic."

Saying goodnight to Sam, we passed through the gatehouse, entered the Colony and walked along the middle of the road.

"Bungalows, bungalows everywhere," I observed.

"That's a line from a poem, isn't it?"

"Not as far as I know."

"Really? It sounds familiar."

There was something not quite real about the Artists' Colony. Or, rather, there was something not quite Kaza about it. What it lacked was the chaos and squalor of the city I knew. Every bungalow was in perfect condition, with no missing roof tiles, no peeling paint, no boarded up windows. Lawns were tidy. Gardens were orderly. It was like a movie set

We strolled down the Rue Picasso. Turned left onto the Rue Duchamp which took us onto the Rue Escher. Halfway down the Rue Escher, the Rue Matisse began.

Number 12 Rue Matisse. Citizen Maxwell's place of abode. Just another bungalow with a tidy lawn.

"Nice place," I said and I meant it.

Citizen Maxwell showed me into her living room and I was genuinely pleased to see her electro-clavier standing in the corner. Where I'd have expected the television to be, there stood a metal palm tree. Framed paintings adorned the walls. About a third were cubist; a third were absurdist; and the remainder were surreal.

"You paint these?" I asked.

"No," said Citizen Maxwell. "I don't find my own work easy to live with."

"Yeah. I sometimes have that problem too,"

"Give me your coat and make yourself at home. I'll fetch the whisky."

Her settee was leather. Leather! In all my life – or at least the life I remembered – I had seen two leather chairs, one leather pouffe and a leather bean bag. This was my first leather settee.

I sat on it and luxuriated in its aroma.

My day had so far consisted of examining a stiff, identifying a mass murderer, arresting an ex-fugitive and going to the flicks with a beautiful woman. But it seemed to me that the most abiding memory of it would be the moment I parked my arse on the tanned skin of a dead animal.

Citizen Maxwell returned minus her jacket and

bearing a bottle of Kaza Sour Mash, a couple of tumblers and a bucket of ice. She kicked off her shoes and joined me on the settee. "You be mother. I like mine on the rocks."

I poured us both a good measure – hers on the rocks, mine with a solitary ice cube. It had been a long time since I'd had sour mash and the first sip brought fond memories.

"I guess this is when you ask me the question," said Citizen Maxwell once we were both good and relaxed.

"And which question would that be?"

"Am I planning on working tonight?"

"That wouldn't be my first question."

"Let me guess. You want to know what a nice girl like me is doing turning tricks on the Rue Dante."

"You live in the Artists' Colony, which means you're a State Registered Artist, which means in turn you pay no rent and get a monthly stipend courtesy of the Municipal Government. You may not be rich, but you're not exactly poor."

"Depends on your definition of poor. You see that machine over there?" She pointed to her electro-clavier. "To build that cost me about the average annual salary of an average civil servant. I know because I had an average civil servant do the sums for me."

"Do you still play it?"

"Not since it stopped working. You were privileged to witness its one and only public appearance – an appearance, mind you, for which I received no payment. Those lousy sons of bitches at the Cafe Voltaire stiffed me good and proper."

"You never tried any of the other clubs?"

"Sure. I even rustled up a few bookings. But they got cancelled when the Musician's Union threatened to picket any place I played. My machine can take the place of an entire orchestra, and they were scared it would put them out of work." Citizen Maxwell picked an ice cube from her glass and ran it along the bottom of her jaw. "And now we come to the second question. *Am I going to be walking the streets tonight?* No, I am not. Nor am I going to be walking them tomorrow or any time soon. It was scary enough when the West Side Ripper was on the loose, but now there's someone even scarier out there."

"There is? Who?"

"The man who killed the West Side Ripper."

Son of Jack. I'd forgotten about him. There was no proof he was a serial killer, but there was no proof he wasn't. If, as I surmised, he was the Ripper's accomplice then Citizen Maxwell was wise to err on the side of caution.

We were on our third drink when I got around to asking question number three. "Why did you come to Samson's this afternoon?"

"You think I came looking for you, don't you? You think I couldn't bear to stay away from you a moment longer."

I squirmed. "Well, no. I wasn't thinking that at all. It's just that – you know."

She leaned forward to flick ash into the pewter ashtray lying between her feet. "For a streetwise, battle-hardened cop, you sure are easy to embarrass. If you must know, I did come looking for you. I thought you'd be good company, and so far you haven't let me down."

"You no longer think I'm an arsehole?"

"You're an arsehole all right. But you make up for it by being decent." She stubbed out her cigarette and turned round so she was kneeling on the settee. "I think it's time I showed you these."

Citizen Maxwell reached behind the settee and pulled out an artist's portfolio. "Here." She placed the portfolio on my lap. "Tell me what you think."

I put my glass on the arm of the settee and opened the portfolio. It was a shock to find myself looking at my own face drawn in pastels. Although well executed, the portrait was hardly flattering, so I didn't spend much time studying it.

The next piece was me again. This time I was sitting at the bar in Samson's, reading, of all things, a paperback. It was a charcoal piece that nicely captured the comforting gloom of the bar's interior.

I flicked through the other sketches in the portfolio and counted twenty-two in all, done in pastel, charcoal, ink, pencil and water colour. Most were of me sitting at the bar or my special table. One showed me standing beneath a street light wearing my raincoat and a trilby hat.

What the hell was I to make of it all? Did Citizen Maxwell expect me to feel flattered?

I studied her face, looking for some hint of smugness, some sign that she was inwardly laughing at me. But all I could see was an impassive coolness that was hard to read.

"I don't like being stalked," I told her.

"I'd hardly call watching someone in a public bar stalking."

"How long have you been doing this? Spying on me?"

"Not spying – observing. And it's been about three months."

"Why in God's name me of all people?"

"There were others before you. Other people in other bars. Even other people in Samson's. And the only thing they had in common was that they were ordinary. I know this will sound pretentious, Inspector, but I don't get much ordinariness in my life. My neighbours are artists – creative types with a bewildering array of eccentricities, quirks and neuroses. Ordinary is a rare commodity in these parts. If I want it, I have to go and find it."

"And you found it in me?"

"Oodles and oodles of it."

Ordinary. Just your average Joe. A face in any crowd. Although less than flattering, it was not a description I could argue with.

Citizen Maxwell shuffled closer. Her thigh was near enough for my own to feel the warmth from it. She smelt of woman, whisky and cigarettes. "When you walked into that bedroom this morning to question me, I thought I'd been rumbled. I could see you thinking you knew me from somewhere, and I kept expecting you to blurt out that you had seen me in Samson's. So it was quite a relief when you mentioned the Cafe Voltaire.

"Even so, I knew our relationship had changed irreversibly. I was no longer invisible to you, so I thought I'd better come clean."

Citizen Maxwell took two cigarettes, placed them between her lips and lit them. She held one in front of my face. "Go on. You know you're going to crack sooner or later. You might as well get it over and done with."

I took the cigarette and for a moment considered stubbing it out. Then I saw Citizen Maxwell draw on hers. I saw the look of bliss on her face. And I saw her breasts rise as she drew the smoke into her lungs. And I was lost.

That first tentative puff after months of abstinence gave me the same sense of relief I get when kicking off a pair of tight shoes.

Tossing aside the portfolio, Citizen Maxwell straddled my lap. "Open your mouth."

"What for?"

"Just do it." She took a drag of her cigarette, waited

for me to obey, placed her mouth close to mine and then blew. "Breathe in."

I breathed deeply, drawing into me (as I saw it) some vital part of her exquisite essence.

The next moments were a frenzy. Our lips didn't so much touch as collide. My hands found their way to the small of her back. Her fingers teased my neck.

I began to unbutton her blouse but was too slow. She gave the garment a violent tug that caused buttons to fly. Then I all but ripped it to shreds.

A glass bounced across the floor as we rolled from the settee onto the rug.

Afterwards, as we lay on the floor, catching our breath and looking like shipwrecked sailors the sea had tossed onto dry land, I was struck by how little noise Cora had made during our love-making. Perhaps that was a clue as to why she called herself the Silence.

Our cigarettes had found their way to opposite ends of the room. They had both burned out but not before leaving their mark on the wooden floor.

Round two of our coupling was more civilised and took place in Cora's bedroom. When we were done, I mentioned out of politeness that I should be heading home.

"Stay," said Cora. "Please."

I stayed.

---

8. Damnation

Another day, another murder.

Citizen Elmore Brecht, cockroach exterminator, sat very much dead in an armchair. White powder clogged his mouth and nostrils. It was also sprinkled on his

face and torso like talcum powder. His killer had
carved the word *LIAR* across his forehead.

"Judging by the paucity of spilt blood," said Gert
Wyman, "I would say it was done post mortem."

There was a flash and a pop as Gene Hooke took a
picture of the fumigation canister standing between
the dead man's legs. "Steady hand," he observed.
"Whoever wrote that must have taken their time."

I gave him a look that told him to leave the detective
work to the detective. He acknowledged it with a
shrug and busied himself photographing the rest of
the apartment. And what an apartment it was.
Although not particularly large – except compared to
my own – it was certainly big enough for a bachelor
like Elmore Brecht to rattle around in. The furniture
and fittings looked new and must have set him back a
fair bit.

The television was about the size of my kitchen
sideboard and the electric gramophone was the very
model I'd been saving for. A few more weeks and I'd be
in a position to make my first down payment.

Just to rub it in, Elmore Brecht was dressed in silk
pyjamas with the letter *E* monogrammed on the shirt
pocket.

When I'd entered the apartment and clocked its
contents, I'd immediately concluded that Brecht was
either a thief or a fence. But then Gene had to go and
burst my bubble by pointing out how much an
exterminator earned and how much overtime they had
access to.

My response was plain. "I'm in the wrong fucking
job."

Just as it had been at the last murder scene, the air
conditioning was switched off, but this time for good
reason. Even in small quantities, roach powder
produces unpleasant effects, and the less of it that got
into the air, the better.

"How sure are you that the powder killed him?" I asked Citizen Wyman.

The fat coroner made a dismissive gesture. "You must have come to the same conclusion about that as I did. There's no sign of a struggle. It looks like he just sat there and let chummy pour poison into whatever orifices came to hand."

"So he was either unconscious when it happened or dead."

"Dead, Inspector. Roach powder causes convulsions when ingested. Even if your man here was unconscious when it happened, he would not be sitting comfortably."

I walked around the armchair to inspect the body from all angles. "So he was poisoned with something other than roach powder?"

"Or he died of natural causes. Who knows?" Wyman leaned towards the corpse. His nostrils twitched. "What's that I smell?"

The fact that he was his usual sweaty self offered an immediate and obvious answer, but I assumed he was talking about the late Citizen Brecht.

Careful not to inhale roach powder, I had a quick sniff. "A curious mixture of lavender and body odour. I would say that Citizen Brecht is – or rather was – one of those deluded types who consider a splash of toilet water a decent substitute for a shower."

"It's not Citizen Brecht I can smell. It's something else." Wyman took a couple of steps towards me and sniffed again. "Yes. There it is. Not just the expected tang of cheap whisky and bacon grease, although they're there in abundance." He stepped back and pronounced in an accusatory voice: "Inspector! You smell of sexual intercourse!"

The constable standing guard at the door sniggered. I made a note to volunteer him for traffic duty.

"Wow!" said Gene, taking my photograph. "Hold the

front page! Inspector Seth Norton gets his end away! Read all about it."

I was saved from having to come up with a witty and no doubt devastating retort by the ringing of a phone in the bedroom.

"That will be the victim's boss," I said, taking a handkerchief from my pocket. "He's no doubt wanting to know why everybody's favourite exterminator isn't at work today."

I hurried into the bedroom and, using my handkerchief to preserve fingerprints, picked up the handset. "This is the residence of Citizen Elmore Brecht. Who's speaking, please?"

"Congratulations, Norton. You've really fucked up this time!" It was the Chief. "Can you imagine the field day the press are going to have when they find out you lied when you told them the West Side Ripper was dead? They are going to rip you to shreds. And when they're done with you, I'm going to glue you back together so I can rip you to shreds all over again!"

"With all due respect, Chief, you're talking bollocks."

This brought the express train that was the Chief's mouth to a screeching halt. I could picture him at his desk, his face as red and hot as the fires of Hell, smoke gushing from his ears, hate in his eyes and all the cogs in his mind thrown out of sync and clashing against one another.

"The Ripper's dead, Chief. Whoever killed him, killed Elmore Brecht. I'm afraid we have a second psycho-killer on our hands."

"Did you just say I'm talking bollocks?"

"Yes, Chief. I certainly did."

"Well, you'd better be right, Norton. You'd better be bang on the button."

The Chief hung up. I expect he went for a nice lie down somewhere quiet.

Gene Hooke was in the doorway. He whistled his

appreciation. "Do my ears deceive me or did I just hear you tell the Chief he was talking bollocks?"

I put the handset back in its cradle. "Nothing wrong with your ears, Gene. It's my mouth that's at fault."

---

9. Cogitation

"First things first," I told Sergeant Studebaker. "We've got to come up with a name for our new killer."

We were in the Incident Room. It resembled a shrine to the West Side Ripper. The walls were covered with maps, photographs, newspaper clippings, notes, drawings, a ticket stub, a lady's glove and an assortment of other so-called clues that had led us astray.

Looking around, I fancied that my head had exploded and plastered the room with all the information in it regarding the Ripper.

"How about the Ripper Mark 2?" Studebaker suggested. "Or Mark 3?"

"3?"

"Well, that bug exterminator who killed the Ripper would be Mark 2. So whoever killed Mark 2 has to be Mark 3."

"Let me explain one more time, Sergeant. Citizen Brecht did not kill the West Side Ripper. He claimed he did but—" I broke off at the sight of Studebaker's stupid grin. "Right. You're yanking my chain."

"Got you real good, didn't I, boss?"

"Yes. Well done. Good show. Ha fucking ha. Now if we could just come up with a name for our new whacko on the block..."

"If this guy really was Jack the Revelator's partner, he ought to be called Jill the Revelator."

"Tell me you're not serious, Sergeant."

"To be honest, that sounded good inside my head. It

was only when I started saying it out loud that I realised maybe not."

"We'll call him Son of Jack for now," I decided. "When the press come up with their own name, we'll go along with that. Now how many men have we got assigned to us?"

"Six – and they're all eager to get things moving. What do you want them to do, boss?"

"To be honest, Sergeant, I haven't the faintest idea."

Lacking a better plan, I sent the team out to go over old Ripper ground. Their orders were to revisit every murder scene, re-examine every bit of evidence and re-question every potential witness. I knew it would do no good, but at least it got them out of my hair.

In the meantime, I took refuge in my office where I planned to spend the day going through the masses of data we'd compiled during our ineffectual pursuit of the West Side Ripper. There had to be something I'd missed, some hint as to who we were dealing with here.

After an hour cooped up in my office, reading and re-reading reports that made less sense each time I read them, I'd had enough. If there was any new information to be gleaned from the reports, I was not in the right frame of mind to spot it.

A couple of slugs of my work whisky really let me down. After a night downing Kaza Sour Mash, the ordinary stuff just didn't cut it.

It was a cockroach that spurred me into action. The little bugger strolled across my desk like he had every right to do so. Annoyed by the insect's insolence, I let him have it with my whisky bottle, bringing it down on his primitive body like a vengeful god.

I missed.

Next thing I knew, I was looking at a broken bottle

and a rapidly spreading pool of spilt whisky. The cockroach was nowhere to be seen.

"Fuck it. I'm going to grab me some culture."

As far as I knew, the Kaza Institute of Contemporary Art was the only completely white building in Kaza. With its five circular levels, each one smaller than the one below, there was no mystery as to why the people of Kaza called it the Wedding Cake.

A sign in the foyer informed visitors that the KICA building was a fine example of Art Deco housing an eclectic collection of art, only a tiny proportion of which was on display at any one time. Entrance was free but a donation of at least five assignats per visit would be very much appreciated.

I dropped a ten cent coin into the donation box and went through.

After a quick and prurient browse of the Degenerate Art Gallery followed by a leisurely stroll around the Faux-Cubist Gallery, I took the lift to the top floor.

The Rotunda, a circular room built of yellow bricks, stood like a wheel within a wheel in the middle of the gallery. By its entrance was a sign: *CORA MAXWELL. "THE SILENCE."*

So far I'd pretty much had the KICA to myself, so I was mildly surprised to find other people in the Rotunda. I counted seven in all: an old couple, three guys with a girl and a middle-aged woman dressed in a kaftan.

Almost as if it had been arranged that way to make some point about the Ages of Man, the old people and the young stood on opposite sides of the room with their backs to each other as they studied and deciphered Cora Maxwell's art.

Kaftan Woman sat in the middle on a circular seat.

She had her eyes closed and appeared to be meditating.

A quick glance at the paintings on the wall reassured me that Cora was every bit as good an artist as I'd supposed she was. About half the pictures were scenes from the desert surrounding Kaza-Blanka, rendered in a naturalistic understated way. The rest were studies of Blanka, the White City.

Had I not known otherwise, I would have assumed the two sets of paintings to be the work of two different artists. The desert scenes possessed a desolate beauty that evoked a sense of loss and loneliness, like I was the sole survivor of some awful apocalypse. They tended towards minimalism with just enough detail to render the scene and no more. It wasn't so much what was in the pictures that made them effective as what was left out.

I could see the silence.

Looking at the studies of Blanka was like looking at the world through a fractured crystal. They were a riot of straight lines, none of them vertical or horizontal. The buildings leaned towards the viewer. Perspective was mocked. Every surface clashed with every other surface, like randomly selected notes struck all at once on an out of tune piano.

The White City, Cora seemed to be saying, should not be. All it serves to do is mock us with our mortality and the limits of our perceptions.

It was brutal, uncompromising art and it was mildly terrifying.

So this was Cora Maxwell, or two facets of her. The desert scenes were all about silence and longing and loneliness.

Once, many years ago, I had spent time camping in the desert on my own. So I knew the uniqueness of its silence. If I could paint, I would paint the desert the same way as Cora.

As to the Blanka pictures: I found myself doing what I did with the city they depicted. I pushed them out of my mind.

Back in my office, I tried ringing Cora but got no reply. Too bad. I wanted her to know I'd been to her exhibition and was thoroughly impressed. I also wanted to make sure she knew I was keen to see her again.

Barely two seconds after I'd put the phone down, it rang. Foolishly assuming Cora would be on the other end of the line, I snatched up the hand set.

"Norton."

"Yeah, Wyman here." The pathologist sounded distracted, as if he was reading while talking. "You'd better come and get your path report – assuming you still want it."

"Send it up to me, will you?"

"Bollocks to that, you lazy-arsed twerp. If you want this report, you can jolly well come and get it."

I was halfway through what would have been the first of many expletives when Wyman cut the connection.

When I entered the morgue, I felt for a moment like I was back at the Kaza ICA. One of the rooms at the gallery, having been made to resemble an operating theatre, had been afflicted with the same white tiles and the same bland lighting that made everything it fell upon look like it wasn't entirely there.

Gert Wyman wore a rubber apron. He stood beside a table laden with grim-looking instruments designed to probe and render human flesh. The tools of his trade.

The wall behind him was adorned with a 5x4 array

of metal doors, any of which may have been hiding a corpse.

He held up a buff folder. "All you ever wanted to know about the late Citizen Anton Delgado," he joked, "but were too afraid to ask."

"Any surprises?" I took the folder and tucked it under my arm.

"Only one, Inspector. Come and take a shufti at this."

Wyman waddled over to his workbench where he had his microscope set up. The only other thing on the bench was the poker found beside Delgado's body. It had been cleaned up and wrapped in clear plastic.

"You recognise this, of course. Your putative murder weapon."

"Putative?"

"You missed all the fun last night. Me and the lab boys spent a happy few hours ramming this puppy into the skulls of freshly slaughtered pigs. Try as we might, we could not replicate Citizen Delgado's fatal wound."

"And yet the poker was found right next to Delgado with bits of his brains on it."

"Looks to me like Delgado was shot at close range with a crossbow or something similar. Our murderer removed the bolt then inserted the poker into the wound, wriggled it about and left it on the floor for us to find."

"So you're saying the murderer went out of his way to mislead us as to the nature of the murder weapon?"

"That about sums it up?"

"Why would he do that?"

"If I had to guess, I'd say it was because he's mad."

---

10. Recreation

Cora wasn't home. I'd tried several times to phone her

from work but with no luck. So now here I was at her front door, ringing her bell and calling through the letter box.

"Can I help?" Cora's next door neighbour had come out to see what the fuss was all about. She was a portly woman with the sort of rosy face you associate with jam and apple pies. "If you're looking for Citizen Maxwell, she's not in."

"Any idea where she might be?"

"I saw her drive off this morning with her easel and paints. She's probably gone off to the desert to do some more of those damnable landscapes of hers. In which case she'll be gone for days if not weeks."

"Damnable?"

"Have you not seen them? The emptiness? The despair? Oh, don't get me wrong. Cora's a great artist – possibly the best Kaza's ever produced, but she does herself no favours by making her work so challenging. Me – I'm only half the artist she is, yet I sell ten times as much work at ten times the price. Why? Because I give the public what the public wants. It's a trick Cora's yet to learn."

"She's got her own room at the Kaza ICA."

"For one week only."

I took out my notepad, scribbled down my phone number and the words *call me*, tore out the sheet and popped it through the letter box. As I headed towards my car, Cora's neighbour called after me.

"You're a policeman, aren't you? Cora's not in any trouble, is she?"

"No," I said, fishing in my pocket for my keys. "I'm a friend."

"Have you ever thought about life modelling?"

"Life what?"

"Posing for pictures. You have an interesting face, Constable. You'd make a great model."

"Constable? I'm a Detective bloody Inspector."

"Sorry. No offence."

Plenty taken. I spotted my keys sitting in the car's ignition. "And what exactly is so interesting about my face?"

"It looks lived in, Inspector."

"Thanks a bundle." I climbed into the car and thought about arresting the woman. Unfortunately, there's no law against being bloody annoying – at least not when you're standing in your own driveway.

I started the car and pulled away. As I headed down the road, I heard a shrill voice: "I'd like to paint you naked, Constable! Call me if you're interested."

An hour later, I was sitting in the Tabula Rasa, a jazz club on the Strip, nursing a whisky and wondering how I was going to get through the night. In my head, I was conversing with an imaginary Cora Maxwell, telling her about my life and my record collection while she gazed at me adoringly.

A cigarette girl came by my table. She had a nice smile so I bought a packet of Kaza Blue Tips. There's something strangely satisfying about opening a fresh packet of fags and peeling off the gold foil to reveal twenty sticks of forthcoming pleasure. After picturing myself offering one to Cora, I teased a cigarette out of the box and placed it between my lips.

Seeing me looking for a light, the cigarette girl hurried to my rescue with a book of matches. I gave her a tip and a wink and she told me I was welcome.

As I drew tar and other noxious chemicals into my lungs, the world suddenly seemed a better place. "Oh fuck," I muttered. "That feels good."

I grabbed a passing waiter and asked him to bring me a large whisky. "As you can no doubt tell," I told him, "I'm a cop, so make sure it's the good shit or I'll have this place raided."

"It's all the good shit," said the waiter, feigning controlled outrage. "We don't water down our drinks – ever!"

I distinctly heard him mutter *arsehole* as he headed for the bar. A minute later, he was back with a smarmy grin and a half bottle of whisky. "On the house, sir. We appreciate all the good work done by the brave men and women of the Kaza Police Department."

"That's nice to hear." I slipped a 10 assignat note into the waiter's hand. "It sure makes me feel all warm and glowy."

Chummy's grin changed from smarmy to something bordering on sincere. "I hope you enjoy your evening, sir."

As it happens, I enjoyed it very much. The music was good, the whisky was bearable and the cigarettes were the icing on the cake.

It was just after two o'clock when I decided I was in danger of having too much of a good thing. I slipped the whisky bottle into my pocket – it was still good for a couple of slugs – and left a tip on the table.

On my way out, I bought another packet of cigarettes from the cigarette girl just so I could see her smile again.

It was a fair old walk back to my hovel, but there's some truth in the saying that whisky gives you wings, and it seemed like my journey took barely any time at all. Along the way, I smoked another cigarette and finished off my on-the-house booze.

As I let myself into the apartment, the phone began to ring. It looked like my night wasn't yet over.

"Bollocks." I kicked off my shoes. "Ring all you like, matey. I'm off to bed."

A phone call at that time of night could only mean Son of Jack had struck again. So bloody what? There was nothing I could do about it that couldn't wait until I'd had a good night's sleep.

I stalked into the kitchen, intent on pulling the phone from its socket. The cord was in my hand and ready to be given a good yank when I remembered the note I'd left Cora. Although I was near certain it was a mistake, I picked up the hand set. "Norton."

"So you've made it home, Inspector Arsehole." It was Cora. She sounded drunk. Sweet but drunk. "Here's a tip for you. When you leave a beautiful woman a note telling her to ring you, you stay by your phone until she does."

"That's very sound advice. I shall remember it."

"So here I am. You bade me ring you and ring you I have."

"I just wanted to make sure you were OK."

"Really? Is that all? And here I was hoping you were intent on ravishing my sweet tender body again."

"Well, that also."

"How soon can you get here?"

"To be honest, I've had quite a skinful tonight. I've just about enough strength to make it to the bedroom. I really am very tired."

"I have some pills that can take care of that. As it says on the bottle, they won't let you down – if you take my meaning. I've left the front door on the latch so you can come in without me having to get out of bed wearing nothing but this skimpy night dress."

"Hang up," I told her. "I need to call a taxi."

---

11. Investigation

How is it possible to wake up feeling so bad and yet so good?

The indulgences that had been a source of joy the night before – the booze, the fags, the pills, the sex –

were now causing me no end of grief. My head and body ached. My heart was working a little too hard for comfort. My eyes stung. My stomach was awash with acid.

And yet I felt so bloody good.

Cora was already up but her essence remained. I rolled onto her side of the bed and breathed deeply of her perfume. She couldn't have been out of bed for long because her pillow was still warm.

Slices of daylight fell through half-open blinds, which meant I was late for work. The thought was a pleasant one. Perhaps I wouldn't show my face at all today. Perhaps I'd let Sergeant Studebaker run the show for a while and see what kind of a fist he made of it. Like all my subordinates, he felt he could do my job better than me. It would do him good to learn otherwise.

I would have stayed in bed a lot longer if the morning calm hadn't been shattered by an abrupt eruption of noise. The whine of an electric motor supplied a discordant undertone to the din of metal attacking stone like a demented woodpecker. Although the racket came from next door, it felt like it was inside my head.

Coffee was what I needed. Lots of it and very soon.

I got out bed, threw on my clothes and sloped off to the kitchen. The smell of freshly perked coffee and the sight of Cora at the table nibbling on toast did wonders for my mood.

Cora smiled up at me. "I had a bet with myself that you'd sleep through whatever Bibi could throw at you. Seems I was wrong."

"Bibi? Is that your neighbour? What the hell is she doing using a jackhammer at this time of morning?"

"She's a sculptress. You must have seen her work scattered around the city."

"Bibi Montague? Is that who she is?" Just about

every civic building and public park in Kaza was blessed with one or more of her abstract sculptures. Impressed, I poured myself a cup of black coffee and held it to my face so I could breathe in its aroma. "I bumped into her yesterday. She wants to paint me naked."

"Make sure she pays you big bucks. She can afford it."

I took a sip of the coffee, bracing myself for a shudder that never arrived. Unlike the crap I was used to, Cora's coffee was smooth and had just enough bitterness to make it satisfying. I wanted to know where I could get some for myself, but before I could frame the question, the toilet flushed in the bathroom.

I looked questioningly at Cora and she gave me a wait-and-see look.

So I waited while whoever was in the bathroom unlocked the door. Sergeant Studebaker wiped his hands on his trousers as he strolled into the kitchen.

"Oh hi, Inspector. I see you're up then. We'd better get going."

I looked even more questioningly at Cora.

"The sergeant arrived just before you showed your face," she explained. "You're wanted on police business."

"Yeah," Studebaker confirmed. "We didn't want you to miss all the fun."

"How did you know I would be here?

"Wasn't hard to figure. Yesterday, you came to work all chirpy so I knew there was a new woman in your life."

"Chirpy?" I was outraged at the suggestion.

"Maybe that's too strong a word. I should have said you were slightly less of an arsehole than usual. And I could smell a faint aroma of perfume on you. Plus that mark on your neck was a bit of a giveaway."

"You couldn't have seen that. I had my top button done up."

"That's what gave it away. You never do your top button up." Studebaker grinned. "How am I doing, Inspector? You still think I'll never make a detective?"

"You want to tell me how you knew the lady in question was Citizen Maxwell?"

"Well now let me see. Maybe it was something to do with you interviewing her in your office instead of the fish tank. Or maybe it was the way you looked at her, which was kind of the way my dog looks at me when I bring it a bone. Don't worry though. Your secret is safe with me and all the other guys and girls at work – and their friends and families."

Cora burst out laughing. "Isn't this where you're supposed to say it's a fair cop or something?"

"No," I said, feeling myself blush. "This is where I insist upon the right to remain silent."

Sergeant Studebaker waited until we were in his car and safely beyond ear shot of Cora before telling me what had necessitated him hunting me down.

"There's been another one," he said plainly. "And this time it's a biggy."

"By biggy you mean...?"

"Hugo Levinson."

"Remind me."

"The Minister for Arts."

I let that one sink in for a couple of seconds, then asked: "And we're sure it's the work of Son of Jack?"

Studebaker started the engine. "Not sure at all."

The air conditioning kicked in. I leant forward to get cold air on my face, hoping it would clear my head. It didn't.

As we headed down the road, I caught myself looking in the rear-view mirror somehow expecting to see Cora Maxwell standing on her doorstep, waving me goodbye. Of course she was doing no such thing.

"You're smiling, sir," Studebaker pointed out. "I don't think I've ever seen you do that before."

I wiped my hand across my mouth and the smile was gone. "You said you weren't sure it's the work of Son of Jack?"

"Not me exactly. Gert Wyman is the Doubting Thomas on this one. He's come up with some theory about how there is no Son of Jack."

"The man's a moron."

"He may be right though. Whoever killed the minister went on to remove his heart, spleen, kidney and liver – and they made a nice clean job of it.."

"So the killer used Jack's m.o.? So what? It's hardly surprising considering he was Jack's partner in crime."

"Or possibly not. Wyman thinks West Side Jack is still alive and responsible for the deaths of both Elmore Brecht and Hugo Levinson."

"That man is so full of crap."

Studebaker pulled up outside a red brick monstrosity. Situated beside the Kaza River, it imitated the architecture of Blanka in a way that almost mocked it. Six storeys tall and with the footprint of a football stadium, it looked like the architect had taken pictures of the buildings in Kaza, cut them up and pasted them back together in no particular order.

The result was as heavy on the mind as it was on the eye.

"Here we are," Studebaker declared. "Paradise Heights. I love this building."

I wanted to thump him. "This is where the Minister for Arts lived? Seriously?"

"Not lived exactly. Unbeknownst to his wife, the Right Honourable Gentleman was renting the penthouse suite as a venue for what you might call his away games."

"A love nest?"

"I prefer the term *shag pad*, but each to his own."

Paradise Heights had a concierge who happened to be an ex-cop operating on the triple principle of *hear no evil, see no evil* and *speak no evil*.

He was not aware the penthouse suite was rented out to the Arts Minister. He had never seen any of the residents, let alone Hugo Levinson, bring home strange women. Just what sort of people did we think resided there?

And as to who might have killed Levinson: our guess was as good as his.

He was a small man with rheumy eyes, a uniform and an attitude. His office was a windowless affair with a hatchway through which he could keep an eye on the foyer. A small bank of television monitors served as windows into other parts of the building. They mostly showed empty corridors.

"The people of Paradise Heights," said the concierge, feet on table, mug of tea in one hand, half eaten sandwich in the other, "pay a lot of money to live here and they expect two things in return. One is luxury. The other is privacy."

"In other words," said Studebaker, "you wouldn't tell us shit no matter what."

"You got it, Sarge. What happens in Paradise Heights stays in Paradise Heights."

"What about tapes? Surely those monitors are recorded?"

"They most certainly are not."

"You're very short," I observed, moving round the desk and looming over the concierge.

He bristled. "Yeah? So what of it?"

"Is that why you left the force? Did they kick you out

when they brought in the new height requirements? Did they turn round and say *Sorry, no dwarves?*"

"I am not a dwarf!"

"What are you then? A midget? A homunculus? A pixie?" I flicked his ear.

"You fucker!" The concierge swung a punch which I almost dodged. It landed with little impact on my upper thigh.

Stepping back, I pulled my gun from its holster and pointed it at his face. "Assaulting a police officer is a serious offence, Shorty. So is resisting arrest."

"I'm not resisting arrest."

"Tell that to the judge. Assuming, of course, you don't get shot while trying to escape."

Shorty looked at Sergeant Studebaker and jerked a thumb in my direction. "Is he always such an arsehole?"

"Not always. Or so I've heard."

"There were wankers like him when I was in the police force. They're the ones who should have been kicked out."

"I couldn't agree more." Studebaker drew his own gun and aimed it in my direction. "Put the gun away, sir. Or I'll shoot you in the bollocks."

"Just whose side are you on?"

"The guy's an ex-cop and we don't go round stitching up our own, do we, boss? Now put the fucking gun away or say goodbye to your love spuds."

I slipped the gun back in its holster. "Have it your way, Sergeant. Just don't go thinking I'm going to forget this."

Studebaker lowered his piece. "You mind if I help myself to a cup of tea?"

"Fill your boots," said the concierge. "But old prune face isn't having any."

"What's your name, by the way?"

"My friends call me Stretch."

The Sergeant gave me a sly wink. "Why don't you go look at the stiff, boss? Me and Stretch would like some privacy."

I headed out to the foyer. As I reached the lifts, Stretch shouted through his hatchway. "You ever point a gun at me again, I'll break your legs. You arsehole!"

The penthouse apartment was a dome. The bedrooms, bathrooms and a few other rooms were arranged around the circumference, leaving what you might call an inner sanctum in the middle.

Most of Hugo Levinson, still technically Minister for the Arts, lay naked on a fur rug that must have been worth a fortune before getting drenched in blood. As to the location of the rest of him – his heart, liver, kidneys and spleen – that was anybody's guess.

"Look familiar?" Gert Wyman taunted as I studied the victim's empty torso with my magnifying glass.

The murderer had cut a doorway into Levinson's stomach, which was exactly the way the Ripper used to do things. "Son of Jack would have known how the Ripper worked. It's no surprise he should operate in exactly the same way."

"Whoever removed those organs knew what they were doing. You don't learn precision surgery by watching someone else do it. Admit it, Inspector: this is the work of Jack the Revelator, aka the West Side Ripper."

"The Ripper's dead."

"Wishful thinking, Norton."

I got up off my knees and stepped away from the corpse. "I'm sure it's not escaped your attention that the deceased is male."

"And?"

"The Ripper's victims were all female and all lived on the West Side."

"Apart from that exterminator chappy and now this chap here."

"Both victims of Son of Jack."

"One hundred assignats says there is no Son of Jack."

"You're on."

Gene Hooke came out of a perimeter room, camera in hand. "Man, this place rocks big time. You should see the bathrooms. They've got gold taps and those things you wash your bollocks in. And the master bedroom! It's got a walk-in wardrobe bigger than my flat!"

I looked around at the expensive furniture and objets d'art and felt an urge to set fire to them. I'm not usually a jealous man but it kind of pissed me off that this hadn't even been Levinson's actual home – just his little playhouse.

"They tell us government ministers don't earn as much as we think," I complained. "It looks to me like chummy here was coining it in beyond our wildest dreams."

"They're all corrupt," Gene chipped in. "Ain't a politician in the entire city who ain't on the take."

Wyman was at the drink's cabinet. "I don't suppose the Minister would begrudge us a drink. I take it you two will join me?"

We took our drinks out onto the roof terrace from where we had as good a view of Blanka as you were ever liable to get from Kaza. From our vantage point, the White City wasn't so white. Fine red sand blown in from the desert formed a barely discernible film on the walls of the buildings. Elsewhere, it accumulated on the roads and pathways and in the courtyards too.

The city was deserted and oh so very quiet.

"The Silence," I said, leaning against the parapet.

Gene and Wyman shot me quizzical looks. I could have told them about Cora's paintings but decided that would be casting pearls before swine. So I said nothing more.

"It's like a ghost," Gene Hooke declared. "A bloody great phantom looming up before us, its nature unknowable, its meaning unclear."

Gert Wyman rattled the ice cubes in his glass. "Bloody awful place. It shouldn't even exist. We should tear it down and bury it."

Footsteps caused me to turn my back on Blanka. Sergeant Studebaker had joined us on the roof.

"Citizen Stretch likes the sound of his own voice," he said with a grin.

"Did you get anything out of him?"

"I sure did." Studebaker shielded his eyes against the glare of the sun and surveyed Blanka. "Now that's what a city should look like. I see you guys have all got a drink. Do you mind if I grab one?"

"Once you've given me your report, Sergeant."

"OK. Here it is in a nutshell. This building has a secret entrance for the exclusive use of the occupier of this here penthouse. It leads to a lift which comes straight to this floor and nowhere else. As far as the tenants are concerned, there ain't no cameras in the entrance or in the lift – except there is. Tucked away in the corner of the lift is a secret camera only the building's owners and security guards know about.

"Anyway, this morning when Stretch clocked on, the guy on the night shift was a bit excited. Thanks to the hidden camera, he'd seen Levinson sneaking a broad up to his shag pad. Nothing unusual in that, of course, except this particular broad wasn't the sort of trash Levinson usually brought home, and the guard recognised her. And you'll never guess who it was."

"The tooth fairy?"

"Bibi Montague, the sculptress!"

12. Deprivation

Studebaker didn't get his drink.

13. Allegation

Bibi Montague wasn't at home. Her latest work in progress – a block of granite the size of a family car – stood beneath an orange tree in her back garden. After careful consideration, I concluded it was most likely the figure of a reclining nude.

Studebaker begged to disagree. "If you look at it from over here and crouch down like this, it don't half look like somebody's innards."

I crouched down, wincing as my knees cracked and a muscle in my back gave a brief spasm of pain, which I took as a warning of worse to come if I pushed my luck. "Still looks like a nude to me."

"See there?" Studebaker pointed. "That's the heart. And there's the liver."

"They're in the wrong place."

"Of course. It's an abstract."

"I don't know. I still can't see it."

"Well, what about those?"

"Buttocks?"

"Lungs."

"They look like buttocks to me. And you can't tell me those aren't breasts."

"They're kidneys, boss."

I tilted my head and crouched down a little bit more. "I think I see a vagina."

"That's because you're a dirty old man."

"Less of the *old*, Sergeant."

We straightened up and studied the sculpture some more.

"I know what you're thinking," I said. "You're thinking Bibi Montague butchered innocent people so she could steal their inner bits to use as models for her sculpture."

"Got it in one."

"She's an abstract artist. Verisimilitude is hardly her stock in trade. Besides which, there are any number of books that could show her what a human kidney looks like."

Studebaker took out his pen knife and opened it. "What do you reckon, boss? Is Bibi the Ripper or not?"

"The Ripper's dead."

"So Citizen Montague is Son of the Ripper?"

"Being seen with Levinson shortly before he was murdered doesn't necessarily make her the murderer."

"So you don't want me to force the back door open with my pen knife?"

"No. I want you to kick it open." Without a warrant, we could only legitimately break into the bungalow if we believed a crime was in process or someone was in imminent danger. Breaking in with a knife would have looked premeditated. Kicking down the door, however, could be construed as two brave coppers going to the aid of a damsel in distress.

Studebaker reluctantly put his knife away. "You have a knack for taking the fun out of things." With as much bad grace as he could muster, he gave the back door a hefty kick. It flew open. "Too easy."

I drew my gun and led the way through to the living room. "Citizen Montague? Are you OK?"

The living room was devoid of furniture. In its place were chunks of stone in various stages of metamorphosis. The floor was littered with carving tools and stone chips.

"And I thought *my* joint was untidy," Studebaker quipped. "I wonder what her bedroom's like."

"Let's go see."

It was tidy and much like you'd expect a middle-aged woman's bedroom to be. There was nothing to suggest we were in the domain of a serial killer.

The rest of the bungalow was a washout. If Bibi Montague was Son of Jack, she had done a mighty good job of hiding it.

Returning to the garden, I looked anxiously towards Cora's bungalow for any sign of either Cora or Citizen Montague.

"Now what?" Studebaker asked as he put the back door back on its hinges.

"Now we pay our respects to Citizen Maxwell and mention in a non-panic inducing way that she might be living next door to a homicidal maniac. Then we put out an APB for Bibi Montague."

Cora didn't answer her door. A quick peep through a few windows convinced me she wasn't at home. Studebaker, however, had his doubts.

"We couldn't see all the way into the bedroom because of the blinds," he pointed out. "And the bathroom window's frosted."

"The air con's off," I countered. "If she was in, it would be on."

"Not if she was dead." Studebaker produced his pen knife again. "I'm assuming she hasn't given you your own key as yet."

"Put that thing away. If she was in, I'd know."

"So now you're psychic?"

I gave Studebaker a look that told him he'd better back off. Thankfully he had enough brains to get the message and put away his knife.

"Yeah, OK. I can dig it," he said as we headed back to the car. "If I had a broad like that, I wouldn't want to risk finding her dead neither."

14. Sedation

The Blue Dragon is the sort of joint you don't know
exists unless somebody wants you to. Halfway down
the Strip, there's a shop that sells records and books.
The room at the back is for scoring whack magazines,
bundles of photographs you wouldn't want your
mother to see and books with titles like *Secretary in
Chains*, *Biker Gangbang* and *Matron's Dirty Secret*.

A grubby curtain hangs in a doorway. Beyond the
curtain is a short corridor that leads to a store room. If
you know where to knock and the exact pattern of
knocks to use, a hidden door opens. Through the door,
down stone stairs, along a passageway and there you
are.

I have no idea how large the Blue Dragon is. It's
housed in part of the Catacombs, that mysterious
labyrinth of vaulted tunnels running beneath the city.
Like many things in Kaza-Blanka, the history of the
Catacombs remains unknown. Rumour has it they had
once been full of human remains and funerary
treasure, all of which was now secreted in a secure
government warehouse. If that was the case, the alcove
in which Cora and I made ourselves comfortable had
to have been a resting place of a more permanent
nature.

Our mattress was stained and the bed clothes were
ragged, but we hadn't come for the decor.

A girl in a blue kimono brought us our first pipe. In
common with all employees of the Blue Dragon, her
face was hidden behind a dragon mask, a consequence
of the joint not having a narcotics licence.

The pipe was lit and handed to Cora, and then the
curtain was drawn. We'd brought along a bottle of
Kaza No. 1 to keep us amused until the opium kicked
in. The smell of the opium was exquisite, like

perfumed marijuana. Cora said it smelt like the wings of burning angels and I wasn't about to argue.

As she drew on the pipe, I noted the glyphs etched into the long stem, which was made of bone or ivory. They were supposedly characters from some forgotten alphabet but I had my doubts. To me they seemed like random yet aesthetically pleasing marks, and I figured they were probably cracks in the bone highlighted with ink.

Cora's face glowed with pleasure. "I love opium," she whispered. "It truly is the stuff of dreams." After handing me the pipe, she cracked open the whisky and took a sip. Then she lay on her side, propped up on her elbow, watching me smoke. "So Bibi's a killer? I find that hard to believe. She's always kind to animals."

"I didn't say she was a killer." I drew some magic fumes into my lungs and felt the first faint stirrings of euphoria. "Just that we need to talk to her."

"You know what I think? I think she's gone to Blanka. I think she'll come wondering back over the Bridge of Sighs with the mind of a new born baby." Cora took the pipe from me and handed me the whisky. "It wouldn't be the first time she's crossed over, you know."

"I wasn't aware of that."

"She's schizophrenic. Going to Blanka seemed like a good way to get rid of the voices."

"A bit drastic."

"But it worked. At least for a while."

We finished the pipe, made love, then ordered another.

As we started on our fifth pipe, we talked more about Bibi Montague and the voices in her head.

"They drove her to seek the Silence," said Cora. "I remember how she was whenever they got too much for her. When she looked at me, it was like there were a thousand people staring out through her eyes, all of them wanting to speak at once." Cora rested her head on my chest. Her breath teased my skin. "Having your mind wiped must be like turning off the music. Only in Bibi's case, there was too much music. It must have been like being surrounded by dozens of radio sets all tuned to a different station.

"Imagine you had a piece of music – a symphony, let's say – and you took away the notes so only the spaces between them remained. Then you'd have silence, but not ordinary silence. This would be *the* Silence – with a capital *S*."

"How would it differ from any other silence?"

"It would remember the music."

Thanks to the opium, I was in an unusually philosophical mood, so I asked, "What if you did it the other way round? What if you kept the notes and got rid of the Silence?"

Cora laughed. "You can't get rid of the Silence. That's why we have music: so we can pretend the Silence isn't there."

We finished off the whisky and smoked a few more pipes of opium.

As I began to slip into enchanted sleep, I heard Cora whisper. "You've been in the desert at night, Seth, and you know how many stars you can see away from the lights of the city. Remove the stars, and you're left with darkness. Only it's darkness with a memory of stars and therefore another manifestation of the Silence.

"It's almost the same with death, but not quite. Death is Silence without memory. That's why it scares us so."

15. Revelation

As the opium dreams faded and my mind tuned into reality once more, there was noise all around me. But amidst that noise, like the space between the notes, there was silence.

Cora was gone.

I checked my watch. It was 7:85, which meant I was already late for work. Cora had mentioned she wouldn't hang around if she woke up before me. Which was entirely sensible. Once the opium's worn off, an opium den's no place to be.

I felt good. Unlike other drugs, opium is a kind mistress so long as you don't abuse her. As I stepped out into the light of day, the city seemed unusually vibrant. The Strip was awash with colours. The traffic sounded musical.

I found a phone box and called the Precinct House to let them know I was on my way. Sergeant Studebaker answered.

"We found Bibi Montague," he said. "She was standing by the Bridge of Sighs. You can guess the rest."

"Is she in custody?"

"She's been committed to Kaza Asylum."

"And her mind's completely wiped?"

"Completely."

"You're sure she's not faking it?"

"The rule book says someone has to question her, so I went along to the nut house to do just that. For half an hour, I sat at her bedside and watched her drool, dribble and defecate. I even went so far as to pretend to punch her in the face; she didn't so much as blink.

"Trust me on this one, boss. Bibi Montague's mind has taken a long vacation."

My mouth was dry, my stomach periodically reminded me it was empty, and I stank of booze, opium and a night at the Blue Dragon. My mind, however, was in good working order.

As soon as I got to the Precinct House, I hauled Studebaker into the Incident Room.

"What are we missing, Sergeant?" I dropped into a chair and put my feet up on a desk. "Let's take it as read that Bibi Montague was Jack the Revelator. We know she was prone to hearing voices, so maybe they told her to kill. And perhaps you were right when you surmised she was ripping out her victims' innards to help her in her work.

"So she prowls around the West Side, picking up loose women from the streets and various gin joints. No one suspects for one moment she might be the Ripper because everyone assumes the Ripper is a man.

"So far, so good. It all makes sense to me until we get to our friend Citizen Anton Delgado, victim number seven. Why did she kill him? He doesn't fit the profile of her earlier victims."

"Perhaps she fancied a change," Sergeant Studebaker suggested.

"No. I don't think that's it. Psycho killers tend to be creatures of habit. Their first kill thrills them so much, they have to keep repeating it. The only thing that varies is the intensity of what they do. Each murder tends to be nastier than the last.

"Bibi Montague killed six women for pleasure or possibly art, but that's not why she killed Delgado. I think that was done out of necessity. Maybe he knew too much."

Studebaker perched himself on the edge of a desk. "I don't think we should trouble ourselves with why Montague snuffed Delgado. The chances are we'll never know, because the one person who could have told us has gone and had her mind wiped."

"You're right, Sergeant. But we're dancing around the elephant in the room. There's one obvious question neither of us have bothered to ask."

"What are the odds against a prostitute picking up a

punter on the very night her neighbour murders him?" Studebaker looked pleased with himself. "Everyone on the team has asked that question, boss. We've been wondering when you'd get round to it."

"That's not the question I had in mind."

"You surprise me."

"My question is how did a middle-aged woman of average build manage to ram a poker through a man's skull? You're the sort of person who chews bricks for breakfast, and I bet even you couldn't do that."

"Actually, it's cornflakes all the way. Not much fibre in bricks."

"Round up a couple of plods and send them to the evidence room. I want everything that was taken from Citizen Delgado's so-called study brought here and laid out neatly on the floor."

"For fuck's sake, boss. You gotta be kidding me. The Chief will go ape shit when he finds out."

"Then we'd better move quickly, hadn't we?"

Studebaker puffed out his cheeks and shook his head. "You know what?" he said. "You're looking at the wrong fucking elephant."

I was fading fast. My night at the Blue Dragon was taking its toll. I needed sleep.

Elephant, elephant, elephant. The word played on a continuous loop in my head. Where was the damned thing?

The items taken from Citizen Delgado's study were laid out in plastic bags on the floor according to where they had been found. The contents of the bookcase were grouped together in several lines, each line being the equivalent of one of the shelves. Everything found on the desk was arranged in a rectangle. And so on.

My innards were awash with coffee. I'd popped a couple of tabs of speed but they weren't having much effect. It was all I could do to keep from sending Studebaker off to fetch me some Quaaludes.

"Do you see a pattern, Sergeant?"

"All I see is a shit load of evidence that's likely to get contaminated."

"There has to be... something!"

Studebaker looked at his watch. "It's nearly lunch time. What say you we get outta here and score some pizza? My treat."

"This is like sheet music. Each bag of evidence is a note of some avant garde jazz piece. You know? The stuff that sounds random but isn't? You ever hear *Principia* by Juice Harris? Its chord progressions are based on pi – 3.14159265359. At first, it sounds like crap, but once you tune into what's going on and pick up the patterns, it both thrills and enthralls."

"Sir, with all due respect, you appear to be talking nonsense."

"The thing is – the thing we have to do is ignore the notes and concentrate on the space between them."

"That's it. I'm off to lunch."

"No, wait! That bag there. The one from the top shelf with the piece of brass in it. You see it? What does it look like to you?"

"I dunno. A piece of brass, I guess."

"And that one there?" I pointed to a third shelf item. It was a mirror image of the first. "And how about this...? And this...? And this...?"

To Studebaker's dismay, I collected up the bags in question and emptied them onto the desk.

"You can't do that!" Studebaker squawked. "You're contaminating the evidence."

"It's only evidence because I had it bagged up. Any other case officer would have left it where it was, but I knew... I just knew..."

"Knew what, boss?"

"I don't know. Let's find out." I shuffled the pieces

about and then slotted them all together. The result was a small crossbow.

Studebaker was impressed. "Bibi Montague was one clever bitch. She hid the murder weapon right under our noses. But there ain't no way she fired a poker with that thing."

"She must have used a normal crossbow bolt and removed it from the victim. Then she shoved the poker into the wound."

"But why leave the crossbow behind? We were bound to find it eventually."

"And a fat lot of good it's done us." I held up the crossbow and admired the craftsmanship that had gone into its creation. There being no weapons factories in Kaza, it seemed likely that Delgado had machined the means of his own destruction. "Citizen Montague wanted us to find this. It's all part of her game – just like her *Dear Pen Pal* letters to me."

Cora didn't answer her phone. When I went to her bungalow, there was no sign of her. Not exactly surprising considering her neighbour's house was cordoned off and swarming with police.

I drove my Kaza Sedan-7 home and parked up outside my apartment building. The place looked grubbier, gloomier and more soul-destroying than ever. It didn't help that a couple of my neighbours were screaming insults at one another or that some joker on the second floor was murdering a song about love tearing him and his sweetheart apart. His weapons were a piano he could barely play and a voice that needed putting out of its misery.

At the top of the basement stairs, I switched on the basement light. It was the cue for a carpet of cockroaches to scarper in all directions and disappear back into the nooks and crannies from which they had come.

Having seen the sight a thousand times, I had almost become inured to it. But my couple of nights in Cora Maxwell's delightful bungalow had opened my eyes somewhat.

It was way too soon for me to suggest moving in with her, but it was definitely on my list of things to do. Of course, Cora might have other ideas, in which case I was quite prepared to take myself down to the Department of Housing and threaten a few people with trumped-up charges unless I got rehoused in something more befitting a detective inspector.

As I entered my apartment, I couldn't help but notice how much it smelt of me in contrast to the way Cora's place smelt of Cora.

A glass of tap water took care of my dry mouth, although I knew it would be only temporary. Coffee was next on the agenda.

I couldn't be bothered to fuss about with the percolator, so I made do with Kaza Instant. Needless to say, it was rank. I drank as much as I could stand then poured the rest into the sink.

So what next? Shower then food then bed? Or food then shower then bed?

A quick sniff of my armpits made it an easy decision.

Twenty minutes later, I was as fresh as the proverbial, shaved, smelling of talcum powder and sporting clean underwear and a shirt that was almost creaseless.

Nothing had happened in the past few days to mitigate the washing up situation. All my cooking and eating utensils remained in the sink, and that's where they were going to stay for now. It wasn't as if there was a shortage of fast food joints in the neighbourhood.

The telephone rang, which put me in a quandary. Not so long ago I'd have put money on the caller being the Chief. But with Cora now in the equation all bets were off.

Should I answer it? Or should I not?

I answered it. "Norton."

"Hey, boss! You made it home then?" It was Studebaker. "Listen; you mind if I come over? Only there's something I need to show ya."

"I'm just about to go grab a burger somewhere. Care to join me?"

"Forget about the burger, boss. Sit tight and I'll be there in a jiffy."

Ten minutes later, I was letting Studebaker into the apartment.

"You must have broken every traffic law in the book," I observed. "My fastest time from the Precinct House is twenty minutes."

"No disrespect, boss," said Studebaker, "but you drive like an old woman."

I pointed at the briefcase he was carrying. "I'm guessing that contains whatever's so hell-fire important it can't wait till I'm back on shift."

"Let's go through to the kitchen. And you'd better fix yourself a whisky. You're gonna need it."

In the kitchen, I fixed myself a whisky and joined Studebaker at the table. As he undid the clasps on his briefcase, the floor trembled.

"Wait a second." I placed my glass in the centre of the table. "Watch this."

I studied the effect on the whisky as the train passed beneath my feet. Unlike the time it had been on the sideboard, the whisky reacted in a random, chaotic fashion, sloshing this way and that and forming nothing resembling a pattern.

Someday I planned to put glasses of whisky all round the apartment and diligently note how they behaved when a subway train came rumbling by. My working hypothesis was that the further the whisky was from the epicentre, the less chaotic would be its behaviour.

The train passed. The whisky settled down. I took a couple of mouthfuls.

"Do you want to know something interesting?" I asked Studebaker. "Something incredibly strange?"

"We gotta get on, boss. This is important."

But I had an unstoppable urge to share what had been playing on my mind ever since I'd moved into the apartment. "About three or four times a day, a train passes beneath my floor."

"So your pad is built over the Metro system? Nothing strange about that."

"Except this is the East Side. The Metro doesn't come this way."

"You sure?"

"I've checked with the Department of Transport. The nearest rail line is in Outer Central, half a kilometre away, and it's elevated."

"Whatever." Studebaker rummaged through his briefcase. "I've been going through the stuff we found in Citizen Delgado's flat and found this." He pulled out a ring binder and handed it to me. "Read it and weep."

It was a set of schematics. I flicked through the pages, each of which contained one or more circuit diagrams. The last page folded out to reveal a picture of a fully-assembled electro-clavier.

"I remember seeing the finished product in Citizen Maxwell's bungalow," Studebaker announced as I handed the folder back to him. "When I asked her about it, she said she'd designed and built it herself. But it turns out that honour actually goes to Citizen Delgado. The two of them weren't such strangers after all."

I finished off my whisky and thought about

ramming the glass into Studebaker's face. Luckily for at least one of us, I decided to refill it instead.

"So Cora told a little fib?" I forced myself to sound civil. "So what?"

"Except it wasn't just the one fib. Last night, while you were zonked out in La-La Land, I checked with the pimps and prozzies on the Rue Dante and ain't none of them ever seen Citizen Maxwell hawking her wares. Which leads to an obvious question. Why would a respectable woman claim to be a prostitute when she's not?" Studebaker reached into his pocket and produced an envelope. "This came for you at the Precinct House. I took the liberty of steaming it open. You need to read it."

I snatched the envelope from Studebaker and re-opened it. Inside was a handwritten letter.

Dear Pen Pal, it began. *All good things must come to an end and this is very likely the last time I will write to you. For me it's been a great deal of fun playing our little game, and I'm sure you've enjoyed it as much as I have. But now it's time for us both to move on.*

Of course, if you'd told me the name of the security guard who'd seen me in the lift with Hugo, then things would be different. I'd have killed him before he realised he had his artists muddled up, you'd have gone on thinking Bibi was the killer, and our game would have carried on a bit longer.

By the time you read this, I'll be airside and beyond your reach. As this is goodbye, I suppose I owe it to you to explain why I killed those people. Firstly, it had nothing to do with their internal organs. I removed those purely as a way of distinguishing myself from the other serial killers that have graced – or will grace – the streets of Kaza-Blanka. Like all artists, I need people to be able to identify my work as my work. By divesting my victims of their hearts, lungs, liver, kidneys and

*wombs, I was signing my name in a cryptic but
unmistakable manner.*

*So why, Inspector? That's the question, isn't it? Why
did I kill all those people?*

*When I die, I want their vengeful souls to be waiting
for me. With them for company, I need never hear the
space between the notes. The Silence shall not have me.*

Yours sincerely.

Jack the Revelator.

---

16. Destination

The sun was setting as Studebaker drove me to the
airport. He wanted to hit the accelerator but I told him
not to.

"There's no point. She's already airside."

"Then there's nothing you can do. Not unless you go
airside yourself and you wouldn't be that dumb, would
you, boss? I mean, now you know she's a psycho bitch
queen from Hell, you ain't still in love with her. Are
you?"

"Just get me to the airport, Sergeant. I'll figure out
what to do when I get there along the way."

We pulled onto the Strip and found ourselves in a
traffic jam. The air was ripe with exhaust fumes and
profanities.

"Do you want me to use the siren?" Studebaker
asked.

"Let's sit it out. Right now, we have all the time in
the world."

I produced my packet of Kaza Blue Tips and offered
one to Studebaker. He took it.

"Why not? I've kinda given up but I couldn't let you
smoke alone. Your head must be in some weird place
right now."

We lit up, smoked a bit. Edged forward a couple of metres.

"I gotta say," said Studebaker, "for a man who's just discovered he's been porking a cold-blooded serial killer, you're holding together pretty well."

"It's the opium. My head's still buzzing." And just as well too. It kept me one step from reality and its accompanying heartache. "I still haven't got it all figured out."

"She played you nicely, boss."

"Anton Delgado was an innocent party. Right?"

"Citizen Maxwell killed him to make you think he was Jack the Revelator and she was his next intended victim. That way she hoped to stop the investigation dead in its tracks. But then Citizen Brecht started bragging about how he'd seen her naked, so she shut him up."

As it so often does in Kaza, the traffic mysteriously unjammed itself and began flowing again. We arrived at the airport just as I was stubbing out my cigarette.

Studebaker pulled up outside the Departures Terminal.

"Tell me you ain't planning to do what I think you're planning to do," he pleaded.

"You'd best head back to the Precinct House and write up what you know. From this point on, you're in charge of the Ripper investigation."

"Think, boss. I'm begging you. If you follow her to Elsewhere, then what? You've no jurisdiction there and she can't be extradited."

"It's my duty to warn the authorities in Elsewhere that they have a killer on their hands."

"Hogwash. This ain't nothing to do with duty and you know it." As I reached for the door handle, Studebaker pulled his gun on me. "I can't let you do this, boss."

I pushed open the door. "The only way you can stop me is to shoot me."

"She was right, you know. You are an arsehole." Studebaker lowered his piece. "'What do you want me to tell the Chief?"

"Tell him I quit and he can go fuck himself. Do you think you can manage that?"

"I'll tell him you'll be back soon – with or without Cora Maxwell."

Studebaker drove off the second I got out of the car. Night had fallen and the airport looked deserted.

I lit up a Kaza Blue Tip and gazed through the perimeter fence at the desert and its big, black sky with its dusting of stars. While Little Moon sailed high in the firmament close to the constellation of Cerberus, Big Moon remained half-hidden by the Kaza Mountains.

I wondered if the sky looked different in Elsewhere.

Patrick Whittaker has made the occasional foray into short film making and has two feature film scripts in pre-production. Two of his shorts – The Raven and Raspberry Ripple – have won awards. He has an honours degree in Media Production. In 2009, he won the British Fantasy Society Short Story Competition with "Dead Astronauts", a tale of odd goings-on in English suburbia. His dystopian novel, Sybernika, is published by Philistine Press: www.philistinepress.com.

Septs

Charles Wilkinson

The boy kicked moodily at the leaves. Anita had swept them into four neat piles, but overnight the wind redistributed them across the terrace, the lawn, the orchard and even as far as the vegetable garden. Should she employ him to collect them up? There would be no point in offering money, though something could be exchanged for his services. She moved closer to the window. In his blue anorak and shiny red wellington boots, he was too well dressed for a feral child. His dark hair fell over his forehead in a fringe, neatly cut in an old-fashioned way. He had a sturdy look and a broad face with healthy red cheeks. No doubt he had come through the hole in the fence that led through to tracts of overgrown land, which had once belonged to the ruinous Victorian villas beyond. Anita assumed the houses had been abandoned, but perhaps a family was subsisting amongst the wreckage. She put on her overcoat and went outside. The boy didn't look up until she was halfway across the lawn.

"Hello," she said.

He made no move to run away, even though he was trespassing. But then, of course, so was she. Observing her progress towards him, he remained perfectly still.

"What are you doing here?"

He studied her with sceptical brown eyes and then turned to look at the house. His clothes had the sheen of the shop on them, as if they had only just been

purchased from a respectable department store –
which was obviously impossible.

"Those windows have glass in them," he said. "That's
clever."

"This is my garden," she lied. "I don't want you in
here unless you make yourself useful."

"Useful. In what way?"

He had stopped looking at the house and was
weighing her up, his eyes wide and watchful.

"See all those leaves? I want you to collect them up,
put them in the wheelbarrow over there and then take
them to the compost heap. If you do that I'll make you
a hot chocolate drink and give you some biscuits.
Would you like that?"

"Can I come into your house? It must be warm in
there. With all that glass in the windows."

She thought for a moment. The boy spoke with no
trace of a regional accent and was neatly dressed. He
was wearing woollen gloves and his shiny dark hair
looked soft and recently washed. Someone must be
looking after him.

"What's your name?"

He stared up at her suspiciously, his lips narrowing
to a slit. She could understand his caution. With the
front line forever shifting, even the most basic
information was best kept to oneself.

"Very well," she said. "I shall call you George. Are
you happy with that?"

"Have you got a rake?"

They went over to the potting shed and she
unlocked the door. There was a smell of earth
accompanied by a faint scent of tomatoes. She handed
him the rake.

"Will you let me come into your house? If I do a
good job..."

"Yes, I suppose so," she said, relenting in spite of
herself. "Are you from over there?

She pointed in the direction of the villas.

But already he had turned away from her and was beginning to rake.

An hour later there was a knock on the door. She put the kettle on the fire before drawing back the latch. He was rubbing his hands together and his cheeks were redder than ever above the lilac line of his lips. She looked beyond him at the garden: the last days of October; a little bedraggled gold clinging to the branches; a huge white cliff of a sky with the scree of a few grey clouds frozen on stone; no hint of colour in the borders. The leaves on the lawn had gone.

"All right. You can come in."

"It's really warm in here," he said, as she shut the door behind him.

"Isn't it where you are?"

"May I sit right by the fire?"

She drew up a chair and watched him holding his hands out to the warmth.

"You still haven't told me where you're living," she said.

He slowly took off his woollen gloves. His hands were raw, chapped, weeping with sores.

"I'm from where it's cold," he said. "Very cold." Steam was rising from him and now there was just a touch of redness in his lips.

An unwashed mug on the table. During the night an intruder had been in the room at the back of the house. She touched the kettle; it was warm. Someone had raked the embers of the fire and added kindling. Yet the windows were intact, and the door into the garden, the only safe way to enter the house, was locked and bolted. Whoever it was had taken the risk of picking a route around the remains of the shattered facade and into the heart of the building, where the walls were ineptly shored up, the floors covered with rubble. A stumble could set off an avalanche of masonry. The one entry into the comparatively undamaged rooms at the back of the house was a hole so small only a child could pass through it. She went through into what was once a dining-room. Lumps of plaster had fallen from the ceiling exposing blast-warped beams, and the wall nearest the front of the building was out of true, its paint work filigreed with cracks. The door into the corridor was locked, its key lost; but scavengers had made a perfunctory attempt to rip out a period fireplace, leaving a gap. She knelt down: long marks in the brick dust where a child had wriggled through.

What had the room looked like when the Chiddingfolds lived there? Differences in the coloration of the bare boards suggested where furniture once stood and rugs were laid. Not a great deal was left in the house when she'd found it; nothing of use, apart from the provisions in the cellar: tinned food, tea, powdered milk, packet soups, cans of cocoa and dried fruit. Most of the personal effects had vanished, but she'd found a drawer with letters and a photograph album in it. No shots of the interior of the house: just the Chiddingfolds on the back terrace. Mother and Father and a teenage daughter with the various guests. The snaps must have been taken before the worst of the disturbances. Their placid middle-class faces and comfortable clothing belonged to an era of contentment and early retirements. Only the daughter's thin nervous face presaged the anxiety of the years to come. In some photographs, she was holding a fudge-coloured Sheltie with a white ruff. It had an inbred, quivering look and was always slightly blurred, the camera incapable of capturing a moment when it was still.

A hammering was coming from the direction of the

garden. This had never happened before. Precipitating a soft shower of dry mortar, she rushed to the back room. George's face, wider and flatter, pressed against the window pane. She unbolted the door, anger and relief competing for emotional supremacy.

"What do you want?"

"It's cold. Can I come in?"

He was wearing a red bobble hat and several brightly coloured scarves.

"You look well wrapped up to me."

"However many clothes I wear I still can't get warm."

The temperature outside had dropped. The last gold leaves curled on the lawn; long bones of silver birch, their ice-scarred branches scraping the frozen sky.

"Well all right. As it happens I've some questions for you."

He was quickly inside and made straight for the fire.

"Did you spend part of last night here?"

"No," he said, glancing up at her. He'd taken off his gloves and was warming his purple fingers.

"Well that's odd because you're the only visitor I've had for many a month. The one person who knows about this fire. That is unless you told someone else."

"I did tell someone."

"Oh, and who was that? A friend, a relative?"

"A brother."

"And this brother. Does he have a name?"

The boy turned his hands over. He wouldn't look at her now.

"All right. This brother of yours. Shall we call him Sidney? Do you think that's a good name for him?"

"Yes, he'd be fine with that."

"And is it possible Sidney could have been in here last night?"

"I think so. You see he's just as cold as I am. Even colder, perhaps."

"And this Sidney he wouldn't by chance happen to
be the same person as George?"

Now he did look at her. There was something in his
eyes she didn't understand.

"Oh no," he said slowly. "We're very different."

The sound of artillery, although still mercifully
distant, was louder today. It was hard to know if this
was because of the direction of the wind or whether
the front line was wavering, the carnage coming closer.

"Well, you make it clear to Sidney he's not to come
in without my permission."

"I'll tell him, but I'm not sure he'll pay much
attention. He's not always the best of brothers."

When George left after lunch, she remembered to
watch him from the back room. He tried the door of
the potting-shed, which fortunately she'd remembered
to lock; then peered in through the windows. He went
over to the outhouse. Its imperfectly attached wooden
staircase led up the side of the wall to an entrance on
the first floor. He put a foot on the bottom step, but
then thought better of proceeding any further. Just
when she'd decided to confront him, he walked rapidly
away and slipped through the hole in the fence.

The motorcyclists swept into the village late in the
afternoon. Although not in uniform, many of them
had rifles slung over their arms; machine-gunners sat
in sidecars or rode pillion. They were heavily bearded
and wore old leather jackets or waistcoats in bright
South American designs. Some sported bandanas or
peaked caps that might once have been worn by naval
commanders. Riding in chevrons, with the leader of
each formation wearing a helmet in the shape of an
animal – a bear, a wolf, a boar – they appeared
simultaneously lawless and disciplined. It was
fortunate that, hearing their growling approach, she

concealed herself in an overgrown hedge on the roadside, where she remained for a good quarter of an hour after the heavy perfume of petrol no longer lingered in the air.

She'd been on her way to the shop to barter tins of beans for a flagon of milk. The route involved walking down a road for a mile with nothing but open fields on either side. If she'd got that far, the motorcyclists would have spotted her; the consequences of which she did not wish to contemplate. Badly shaken, she made her way back to the house. She would wait for nightfall before going to the shop.

It was almost dusk when she slipped back through the side gate that led into the garden. Someone small with his back to her was standing by the potting shed and peering inside.

"George?"

The boy turned round. He was holding a sharp object, possibly a chisel. The door of the potting shed was wide open. As she drew closer, she saw the glint of the broken lock on the ground. George was dressed in a blue boiler suit and had a red handkerchief knotted round his neck.

"George, why have you broken into my shed?"

"My name's not George."

"Perhaps not, but it's what I've been calling you."

"You should be careful how you name people. The results aren't always what you expect."

"I see. Are you Sidney this evening?"

"I don't care what you call me. It won't make any difference to who I am."

"Maybe. But that doesn't explain why you've broken into my property."

"It isn't yours. We were watching you when you moved in about a year ago."

"That's beside the point. You're in my garden now, not a year ago."

"Boundaries move."

His shoulders looked broader in the boiler suit; his legs were planted wide apart on the ground – a little Viking just off his long ship, gazing around for what to plunder first.

"It would be better if you were to go away and come back as George. Then we can discuss this sensibly, Sidney."

"Aren't you are going to do something about your visitor?"

"What visitor? You're the only I can see."

"She's in there. Making herself at home."

Anita turned round. Dancing red and orange light filled the window nearest the fire, which had been out when she left.

"I'll think I'll have that for the time being, Sidney."

To her surprise, he put the chisel straight into her outstretched hand. She made herself walk very calmly across the lawn. The door swung open easily. Anita recognised her at once. Her hair was unkempt and streaked with grey, but the long sensitive face, which was at odds with the world even when it had been a great deal safer, was unmistakable. The woman had moved the most comfortable chair nearer the fire. She was shivering in spite of the warmth of the fire and the tartan rug arranged over her shoulders.

"Miss Chiddingfold?" Anita asked.

The hole in the wooden fence was wide enough for an adult to squeeze through. On the other side, the boy had beaten a way through the ferns, nettles and foxgloves, exposing layers of pine needles beneath. Dank evergreens rose all about Anita; the canopy obscured by November mist. She'd ventured in this direction on one previous occasion; then it had been a fine summer's day. As she pressed deeper into the woodland, the conifers massed about her. The path dwindled to a narrow track. She was about to turn back when she emerged into an open space. In front of her was a derelict swimming pool, with a foot of water at the bottom and assorted debris: old mattresses, a car wheel, a metal tripod that might have been used as the mount for a machine gun, an iron bedstead. Grass and weeds had broken through the roof of the bathing hut. Beyond it the lawns led up to a red-brick villa, cratered with shell holes, its wrought iron balcony askew. Almost the entire upper storey of the building had been blown off, leaving a solitary blackened chimney. Anita knew from her previous visit that the other buildings were in no better condition. Yet George, and whoever was looking after him, must be living somewhere close.

A distant white sun was dispersing the mist. She walked round to the front of the building. An overgrown driveway enclosed a lozenge of seedy grass before leading off through an enormous archway of rhododendrons. Possibly there was a lodge or gatehouse at the other end. If she could speak to whoever was looking after George, a *modus vivendi* might be reached.

The rhododendrons had joined over the driveway, creating a dark crypt. The mosses covering the tar macadam softened her footfalls. It was colder than before. There was a smell of damp and leaves. As yet she could see no light at the end, though it was possible the driveway curved round. About her, the reign of the rhododendrons seemed ever more complete; the darkness so dense she could barely see more than a few paces in front. Then a susurration in the undergrowth, followed by rustling. Whatever was moving about was quite large. A bright beam of light right in her face; in the bushes a human form that for an instant appeared to be holding an enormous white star.

"Oh it's you."

A boy's voice.

"Who is it?"

"It's George. For a second, I thought you were Sidney."

Anita wanted to say that Sidney-George could not be simultaneously by the potting-shed and skulking in the bushes, but she was too relieved to have encountered nothing more dangerous than the boy.

"Would you like to see what I've been doing?"

"If you wish."

He lowered his torch and beckoned her forward. As she crouched to enter the cavernous space he had cut in the rhododendrons, she caught a glimpse of his face; he was wearing his bobble hat. Inside was a small wooden table with a vase of flowers on it. He turned the light on the ground. A number of distinctively coloured stones had been pressed into the earth.

"What's this?"

"It's going to be my special place. For the religion of me. I've told Sidney about it and I think he's jealous, even though he hasn't even seen it."

"Will this religion involve believing in anything? Apart from yourself?"

"I don't know. I haven't quite decided. It's really stupid of Sidney to make such a fuss about my religion when I haven't got very far with it. Anyway, he'll have to make up one of his own. We all will. It's because we're the same that we've got to have different ones. It'll be a way of telling us apart and is bound to lead to a sense of national identity. Sidney says his religion will involve plenty of sacrifices."

A faint click and the torch went out. A deathly sweetness in the air mingled with the scent of earth.

She was inside a cell of dark honeycomb, longing for light and flowers.

"Why have you switched the torch off, George?"

"We're running short of batteries. Sidney says you have a new friend."

"Yes, I suppose I have."

"So there's less room in your house now. If that woman is sleeping there."

"Will you turn on the torch?"

The light came on, less dazzling. She saw the boy had assembled a collection of gardening implements: spades, shovels, forks and what looked very like the rake from her potting-shed.

Anita bent down slightly. George's eyes: unfathomable holes in a yellow mask.

"Will you introduce me to your parents?"

Again, he switched the torch off. She stretched out her hand, aiming to touch his shoulder reassuringly, but he must have moved silently away.

"George!"

"I'll switch the light on if you want to get out."

"All right. I'll go. But just promise you'll introduce me to your parents."

"Can't."

"Why not? Are they dead... injured?"

"They were used up."

What do you mean by that?"

"All their flags and songs. Gone."

"That makes absolutely no..."

The torch beam right in her eyes, blindingly close. He must have crept up on her, without so much as a snap of a twig.

"Do you want to leave now?"

He shone the torch on the entrance and then pointed.

Once or twice she turned round. Was he following her soundlessly? A dim grey light in the distance. Now she had her bearings she began to run-walk and then run. More quickly than she had expected she was outside. The sun had gone; a faint blue mist lingered in the air like gun-smoke. A boy in a boiler suit was sitting on a bench and whittling a stick with an enormous knife. He looked up.

"Have you seen George?" said Sidney.

She took the photograph album out of the drawer and pushed it across the table to Jane Chiddingfold. While the woman turned the pages, Anita put the kettle on the hob and another log on the fire. Outside, night soaked the lawn, the woods and the fence, transmuting subdued drenched greens and browns to leaden weights that pressed dim watery colours up into the sky

Though she made no noise, Jane's face was streaked with tears. Theirs was the age of silent weeping, thought Anita; the subjugation of sound that ensured survival. A scream stifled left one anonymous in the bushes whilst mayhem continued its work on the lawn.

"So this is how you knew my name," said Jane, looking at captioned birthday parties, the dated summer excursions.

"There are some letters too."

Anita wanted to ask her what she'd been through, but it was wise not to ask questions too soon. Although they both spoke standard English, there was no knowing whether their loyalties were to different kingdoms. And her name, Chiddingfold – Anita hadn't come across that before. The letters were personal and gave no indication of the family's allegiance.

"The boy I mentioned. I don't suppose you happened to see him while I was out?"

"Yes, I did. But in fact there were two of them. Dark-haired and very alike. Identical twins."

"Were they messing about in the potting shed?"

"No, they were over there," said Jane, pointing in the direction of the outbuildings. "The old granary seemed to interest them. The top half was a flat years ago."

The staircase was probably strong enough to hold a child's weight. Why was she more frightened now she knew there were two boys than when she'd assumed the existence of one boy with some sort of split personality? Perhaps because she had thought the whole idea of the mischievous twin had been hers.

"Did you speak to them?" asked Anita.

"No, I've learnt to keep well away from children. I don't like to say this, but if the leaders catch them early enough, before they've developed a conscience, you can train them to do..."

"I know. Just about anything. Those two are not telling me their names and I've no idea where they come from. Their accents are pretty... neutral." And just like yours and mine, she thought.

"Are they armed?"

"Knives, as far as I know."

The hammering started as Anita passed a mug of steaming cocoa to Jane. There were no faces pressed to the window. Anita put the door on the chain before opening it.

Two boys were standing outside. In the light from the fire, she could see their dark hair and the impassive match of their features. They were dressed in parkas and jeans.

"We're your new neighbours," announced one of them, in a voice that could have been George's... or Sidney's."

"It's very cold where we come from," the second boy chimed. "Can we come in?"

Low-flying Northumbrian jets; a drone that could have
been anybody's; the sound of mortar fire audible in
the easterlies; wounded motorcyclists retreating to the
Marches, some on foot; farm trucks carrying troops to
relieve Leicester: the return of the heptarchy, though
the borders still fluid – the lines' constant movements;
shifting landscapes plumed with fire and gun-smoke;
territory too provisionally held to be mapped.
Sentence fragments – in her mind all morning.

Anita sat by the fire, turning the dial, finding
maverick channels on air for an hour before they faded
to a crackle; no signals for the television and the
internet down. Making a patchwork of information
from propaganda, and hearsay, trying to create a
picture of events with some relation to the observable
facts.

"You must have known the people on the hill – in
the villas?" she said.

Jane nodded. "Yes, of course. Some of them were
close friends." She turned away and walked over to the
window. "We thought ourselves very lucky we'd had
the sense to get down to the cellar before the worst of
it." She started to draw a shape on a fern-whitened
window pane. "There's no one left in the village, but
you say someone's running a shop at the farm."

"You can exchange goods there. But he won't take
coins, or even silver and gold."

"Do you know who's running it?"

"A middle-aged man. Balding. Quite stocky. I didn't
ask his name."

"I think I might know him."

"He sounds as if he might be a local."

"I'll go there and check it out."

"I'd wait until after dark if I were you. You never
know what's going to come along that road."

"Don't worry. There's a short cut across the fields."

At noon Anita went out onto the front lawn. Once pale gold leaves were damp and dark, slippery with mud and rainwater. She'd forgotten to ask George to return the rake. There were signs of activity in the potting shed and the granary. At least four of the boys were in residence now. Jane had said that she'd help to get them out.

Just as Anita was about to go back inside, George wriggled through the hole in the fence. He beckoned to her impatiently. She signalled to him to come to her but he stayed where he was, his gesticulations becoming ever more urgent.

She made her way across the lane with studied indifference. "What?" she said curtly, as soon as she was close enough to him to avoid raising her voice.

"You've got to come. It's your friend."

"What about her?"

"Quickly," said George. Once she was through the gap, he started to run ahead.

Now she knew the way it seemed a short time before they reached the swimming pool. George pointed at the bathing hut. "In there."

Jane was stretched out on the floor. Blood trickled from her left ear. A spanner matted with hair lay beside her.

"I'm sorry," said George, "but Sidney said she wasn't part of his plans."

Anita knelt down. There was no pulse. Perhaps the previous night they should have let the boys in. Given them cocoa. It was Jane who had been adamant, shutting the door and shouting when their hammerings resumed. But would it have made any difference? After all, this was Sidney's work.

"I'll go and get the spades, but you'll have to say some words. I haven't made up a funeral service yet," said George.

How many hours passed before they returned

slowly, their clothes stained with earth? It was still light when they reached the lawn. The sound of banging and boyish voices arguing from an upstairs window was what she noticed first.

"What are they doing in there?"

"Don't worry," said George. "They're all fine about you coming in. Even Sidney."

This time she ran ahead. She could hear George following close behind. The door to her bedroom was wide open. All her property had gone; the place was a demonic dormitory: a boy giving another a Chinese burn; one who had been thrown off a bunk bed screaming. Although heat was rising from a forge, the walls were white with frost. How many boys were there?

"We're only play fighting at the moment."

Sidney was standing opposite her. He was wearing his boiler suit and carrying a dagger from which an icicle depended like a second blade.

"You can't move in here!" she yelled.

"We need the living space."

"And what have you done with my possessions?"

How could the room be both concurrently very hot and extremely cold? The burning interior of an iceberg? What was it that Jane had said, after she'd slammed the door on the two of them: "Don't you see they've got ice on their shoulders?"

Again, Anita started to count. But when she turned round, there was no sign of George and his red bobble hat.

"How many of you are there?"

"Just seven," said Sidney.

Two boys were wrestling darkly with each other in the far corner of the room, a spot so occluded their struggle might have been taking place in a different age.

"Where's George?"

"Not here. He may join us later."

"What's your real name, Sidney? You can tell me that now, surely."

"Kent," he said. "My name is Kent."

"And George?"

"You're right about that. His name is George."

A boy put his arms around Kent, companionably at first. As she watched, the newcomer started to squeeze, tighter and tighter. A chant rose in the room, rhythmic, war-loving, straight from the cold north. Spear, shield, song; sing! shield! spear! The playing was over; the fight began: the strokes slow but terrible; the cuts through the nerve roots, deep into the bone. She turned round once on her way to the door. The boiler suit was changing colour, blue to pink, pink to scarlet; soon there would be one body with two heads. And then one boy, stronger, sanguineous through conquest: one colour on the map. In the background, the other boys struggled like countries, their muscles flexing borders that moved through the centuries.

More songs now, merging with her thoughts, breaking sentences into clauses; phrases to words, kennings. Metal glowed in the forge: flash of the one-edged blade. Dig up weapons from the graves! Worship midwinter, sky, thunder, harvest! Rename the swords: bone-hewer, breath-scald, dream-slayer, skull-cleaver, split-curse, screamer, hope-cutter, roarer!

Historical note: the Heptarchy is a term used to designate Anglo-Saxon kingdoms during part of the period sometimes known as the Dark Ages. The kingdoms, which subsequently became England, were East Anglia, Essex, Kent, Mercia, Northumbria, Sussex and Wessex.

*Charles Wilkinson's publications include The Pain
Tree and Other Stories (London Magazine Editions)
and Ag & Au (Flarestack), a pamphlet of his poems. His
stories have appeared in Best Short Stories 1990
(Heinemann), Best English Short Stories 2 (W.W.
Norton, USA), Unthology (Unthank Books), Best
British Short Stories 2015 (Salt), London Magazine,
Under the Radar, Prole, Able Muse Review (USA), Ninth
Letter (USA) The Sea in Birmingham (TSFG) and in
genre magazines/anthologies such as Supernatural
Tales, Horror Without Victims (Megazanthus Press),
Rustblind and Silverbright (Eibonvale Press), Phantom
Drift, Bourbon Penn, Shadows & Tall Trees, Prole,
Nightscript and Best Weird Fiction 2015 (Undertow
Books, Canada). He lives in Powys, Wales, where he is
heavily outnumbered by members of the ovine
community. A Twist in the Eye, his collection of strange
tales and weird fiction, is forthcoming from Egaeus
Press. Several of the stories first appeared in Theaker's
Quarterly Fiction.*

The Quarterly Review

Reviews by
Stephen Theaker,
Douglas J. Ogurek
and Jacob Edwards

Douglas J. Ogurek's work has appeared in the BFS Journal, The Literary Review, Morpheus Tales, Gone Lawn, and several anthologies. He lives in a Chicago suburb with the woman whose husband he is and their pit bull Phlegmpus Bilesnot. Douglas's website can be found at: www.douglasjogurek.weebly.com.

Jacob Edwards also writes 42-word reviews for Derelict Space Sheep. This writer, poet and recovering lexiphanicist's website is at www.jacobedwards.id.au. He has a Facebook page at www.facebook.com/JacobEdwardsWriter, where he posts poems and the occasional oddity.

Audio

Journey into Space: Frozen in Time, by Charles Chilton (BBC Audio/Audible)

This fifty-seven minute adventure is the fifth *Journey into Space*. The first three, *Operation Luna*, *The Red Planet* and *The World in Peril*, were long, episodic sagas broadcast in the fifties, while the last three, *The Return from Mars*, *Frozen in Time* and *The Host* were radio plays broadcast in 1981, 2008 and 2009 respectively. All were written by Charles Chilton, except *The Host*. As this story begins the usual crew of Captain "Jet" Morgan, "Doc" Matthews, Mitch and Lemmy are on their way back from Neptune in the *Ares*. The cast is all new except David Jacobs, who played several supporting characters in the original trilogy, often in the same scene, and here plays Jet Morgan. A problem with his cryogenic sleep unit meant Jet has been awake for practically the whole thirty-year trip home, and a good thing too or the ship might well have been destroyed. He wakes the others as they approach Mars, long-forgotten and short on fuel. They land near the *Saviour 1*, itself stuck there after developing a fault. Good thing Mitch is here, since in this distant future of 2013 it's unusual for a crew to include an actual engineer. The media rep and the health and safety officer aren't much good at fixing spaceships. The captain is now a "flight manager", and Doc notes with bemusement how the remaining crew of the *Saviour 1* spend all their spare time playing games on their screens. (If Charles Chilton could see us now!) They seem unwell, and there are clues to suggest that they've been up to no good... This story keeps the mood of the originals very well, remarkably so given the fifty years that had passed when this was produced, and that's helped by the use once again of Doc's diary entries to bridge narrative gaps. The crew all behave in recognisable ways, even down to the flashes of the old irritation with each other at times of stress. It's just a shame that it stops after one hour, instead of ten. *Stephen Theaker* ★★★★☆

You're Never Weird on the Internet (Almost), by Felicia Day (Simon & Schuster/Audible)

This is the story of how a badly home-schooled violinist grew up to become a god among the virtual geeks. The face of Felicia Day will be familiar to many more people than actually know who she is; she had a spell as the background photo of some YouTube apps, she sang viral hit "Do You Want to Date My Avatar?", and had eye-catching guest spots in *Buffy the Vampire Slayer*, *Dollhouse* (the episodes set in the future) and *Supernatural*, where her red-headed hacker is the fun kind of friend Sam and Dean badly need in their ever-tortured lives (the episode where they join her at a fantasy battle re-enactment is a classic). Understandably, this book focuses more on her own creative achievements, though it does give us a striking portrait of what it's like to be a struggling (and then a doing-fairly-well) actor in Hollywood. Before that, and after an introduction by Joss Whedon in which he sounds remarkably like Ultron, listeners learn about Felicia Day's childhood, where a miscalculated attempt to get out of some religious nonsense led to her mum withdrawing her from a good school, her education going badly astray from there until violin skills got her a college scholarship at the age of fifteen. Though fierce competitiveness made her the college valedictorian, she didn't love the violin enough to make it her life, and so began her acting, and eventually a desire to write her own scripts. One of the

most interesting parts of the book describes the
support group of aspiring women she joined, and then
constantly lied to about the progress on her script: the
pilot episode of *The Guild*, which would eventually
become a successful web series. It's only after she
comes clean about her fibs, and her addiction to *World
of Warcraft*, that the dam breaks, the members of the
support group become her producers, and the
programme ends up a huge Xbox-endorsed success. It's
a good story, and it's bracing to hear all the hard work
that went into Day's success, as well as all the failures
that led up to it. Later in the book comes a dark period
after she takes on too much, develops health
problems, lets people down, and loses good friends,
but there's always the sense that she's determined to
do the things she wants to do, and any bumps in the
road are eventually going to get flattened. The

penultimate chapter is about her well-publicised run-ins with online boors, which events are all the more unfortunate given the positive light in which gaming (*WOW* aside) and the internet are seen throughout the book. Overall, it's funny, rather inspirational, and sweet-natured, in a steely sort of way. The highlight, I think, is an excruciating scene where a fan recognises her in a build-a-bear workshop, leading shoppers who don't know who she is to act as if she's impudent for being recognised. *Stephen Theaker* ★★★☆☆

Books

Elektrograd: Rusted Blood, by Warren Ellis (Summon Books)

A private eye with a habit of shaking down his clients has been murdered in Mekanoplatz, the northernmost district of Elektrograd, the city of the future, or at least it was, back in the early twentieth century. The idea was that it would be an experimental city, where new forms of architecture and living and work could be tried out. In Mekanoplatz the buildings can walk, reconfiguring themselves to meet new manufacturing needs. They're in the middle of a change now, though homeless people remain where they are, living in the hollowed-out carcasses of abandoned construction robots. Even a beat this dead has a cop who cares: Detective Inspector Ervin Stross, driving an old car that could explode at any time, trailed by a rookie and an ambitious detective sergeant. Behind the murder lies a mystery, and it's a mystery that doesn't want to be uncovered. This is a good novella by a writer better known for his comics like *Transmetropolitan* and the immensely influential *The Authority*, but he spins a good story in prose too. This is like a science fiction version of a satisfying episode of *Columbo* or *Luther*. Warren Ellis's original plan was to write a novella in each region – hope he finds time to write them. It would be great to see more of Strauss's investigations in this fascinating city. *Stephen Theaker* ★★★☆☆

a SUMMON BOOKS fiction edition

ELEKTROGRAD: RUSTED BLOOD

by Warren Ellis

How a Ghastly Story Was Brought to Light by a Common or Garden Butcher's Dog, by Johann Peter Hebel (Penguin Classics)

This fifty-three page book manages to pack in twenty-six short stories, as told by Your Family Friend. The back cover describes them as "fables, sketches and tall tales", but it may remind readers of *The Real Hustle*, which showed BBC viewers how con artists separate the greedy from their money. These stories would have performed a similarly useful duty for the readers of the eighteenth and nineteenth century, stories like "A Stallholder Duped" and "The Weather Man" showing the kind of tricks people might play. Two favourite stories of mine were "One Word Leads to Another", in which a man asks what has been happening at home, and, as is so often is the case, the answer "Nothing much" turns out to be an understatement, and "A Secret Beheading", a strange and terrible tale in which an executioner is kidnapped by unknown parties to do his usual work in a private matter. The back cover tells us that one of these twenty-six stories was Franz Kafka's favourite, but doesn't say which – that one, or perhaps the title story, about a pair of two-time murderers, would be my guess. Hebel writes, at least as translated here by John Hibberd and Nicholas Jacobs, much like Rhys Hughes, albeit without the fantasy. See especially "Strange Reckoning at the Inn", where three clever students try to convince a cleverer-than-they-think pub landlady that since time is a circle and they do not have money to pay their bill, she should be patient and wait for them to return in six thousand years with the money they owe. She points out that they still owe her for the meal they ate six thousand years before. *Stephen Theaker* ★★★☆

Savages, by K.J. Parker (Subterranean Press)

"The end of the world began with a goat..."

Savages, for want of better terminology, is a down-to-earth epic historical fantasy wherein a once-mighty empire hangs in the balance, its waning existence threatened by not-so-proverbial (in fact, ever-so-practical) barbarians at the gate. K.J. Parker threads together several storylines in exploring this scenario, primary of which are those of Raffen, a chieftain whose loss of identity affords him freedom to turn his hand to any craft; Calojan, an imperial general with a self-fulfilling reputation for invincibility; and Aimeric, a pacifist turned arms-maker and politician, upon whose wiles may rest not only the future of the city but also a watertight case for prosecution by cosmic irony. Parker avoids playing favourites, and so each player holds the reader's sympathies in conjunction with the spotlight, this perspective switching subtly whenever one is placed in opposition to another. Such protagonistic ambiguity – a load-bearing device that feeds credence back into the narrative mechanism – is a feature of Parker's novels, and allows the possible storylines to unfold without prejudice. Whatever happens will happen.

In truth, the course of any great event – even such that is studied for centuries afterward and which cruels the future for whole swathes of the population – is shaped not only by the actions of a select few but also by the blind impetus of the many, not to mention fickle and incalculable pieces of happenstance. Evidently, Parker is aware of such nuances and has tasked herself with turning up the specific nail in want of which the battle was lost (while furthermore digging deeper to the botched trade agreement behind the cranberry shortage from which sickened the child of the farrier who failed then properly to shoe the horse in question). That she can do this without losing the story's thread – that her eye for the minutiae presents as a blessing, not a curse – speaks wonders for her authorial craftsmanship.

Far beyond any non-fantasy setting, K.J. Parker's invented worlds are rendered with a faithful eye to the details of real life, their depiction easily outshining those primary accounts of Plutarch, Pliny, Polybius and the like. Whereas other writers – be they concerned with fact or fiction – tend overly to focus on one particular agenda, Parker clearly partakes of a fascination for the practicalities of history, and so concocts for us political intrigue and military operations that remain bound by societal, religious and economic constraints, written not just from the perspective of those who ruled or prevailed but rather

from the varying points of view of everyone involved. We have in evidence moth-eaten shades of Rome (in decline), a sombre nod (and a wink) to Hannibal, horn-blown echoes of Alexander (a goat herder made good), and a veritable potpourri of lesser-known archetypes all adding their pungence to the sensory mix and bringing to life a tale well-grounded in history's truths.

So with such fare on offer, what need now could we have of Appian or Arrian, Tacitus or Thucydides? Why ever would we keep doting on Herodotus, swatting up on Suetonius or paying even lip service to Livy? Why indeed. When K.J. Parker came into being – the dark alter ego of comedic novelist and erstwhile classical scholar Tom Holt – thousands of ancient historians must have thrown their copies of *The History of the Decline and Fall of the Roman Empire* into the air and started dancing the Funky Gibbon (volume after volume) in rapturous peer review. Holt's Parker persona is at once worldly and learned, curious yet cynical, from which outlook *Savages* emerges as a sardonic, slow-burning delight: an immersive page-turner wherein magic plays no part, the fate of empires turns on the veracity (or otherwise) of human endeavour and Parker sets a new high-water mark for authenticity in historical fantasy. *Jacob Edwards*

The Shepherd's Crown, by Terry Pratchett (Harper)

A Wickerword basket.

Terry Pratchett – author and humorist; a writer of such immense popularity, his books for many years topped Britain's most-stolen tally; the man who armed Death with laconic wit and a scythe and made him a recurring character – is dead. This of course was inevitable. THERE CAN BE NO EXCEPTIONS. But for all that Pratchett's passing will leave a vacuum to be filled in

the *New York Times* bestseller lists and the reading
lives of millions of devoted followers, let us not mourn
overmuch; rather, we should cherish the years he gave
us and scrump one last time from the verdant pages of
a new Discworld novel: a gentle, bittersweet
celebration.

Published posthumously, *The Shepherd's Crown* forms a fitting curtain call, not least of all because it commences – not ends, mind you – with the death of Granny Weatherwax, a founding figure in Pratchett's development of the Discworld and a personage whose absence is felt markedly by all around her. If not a knowing postscript (Pratchett never stopped writing and had ideas slowly coalescing into several more novels), having the mantle of head witch pass from Granny Weatherwax to Pratchett's young-adult protagonist Tiffany Aching at very least seems an apposite way to have signed off. Terry Pratchett gave us wizards and watchmen and a weird and wonderful world ever growing with its readers. One might suspect, however, that he always held a soft spot for the witches first introduced in *Equal Rites* (1987), and increasingly in later years for Aching, a hard-working wunderkind who perhaps more than anyone embodied the magic to be found in common sense.

One hallmark of Terry Pratchett's writing is that he was ever inclusive, never patronising. Hence, when the age of his central character denoted young adult fiction, he made no change to his narrative voice – if anything, he tackled slightly more adult themes – and when he structured a mystery, one always had the impression he was feeling his own way through it as well, not merely stringing the reader along. It is appropriate, then, that in a postscript to this last book, Rob Wilkins (Pratchett's assistant) openly acknowledges that *The Shepherd's Crown* was at the time of Pratchett's death still a work in progress. Pratchett, it transpires, would first fashion the bones and then flesh out each story, and this explains why *The Shepherd's Crown*, somewhat thinner than others of Pratchett's works, feels ever-so-vaguely unfinished... but only in the middle! The tale is told, yet we remain witness to the interrupted sparkle of a magic at play. Again, this seems apt.

Terry Pratchett wrote comedic fantasy where much of the humour derived from observations of the everyday and from inviting his audience to recognise their own lives in amongst the Discworld's heady mix. Thus, just as Tiffany Aching finds strength in being grounded to the well-trodden soil of the Chalk, so too do Pratchett's books offer strength through their grounding in truth. The result is dreamy escapism mixed with a pragmatist's droll mirth: uniquely compelling and poignant – enchanted as much as enchanting – and with the power to assimilate both death and Death alike and reconcile them with life. Thank you, Terry, for sharing your gift these many years. *Jacob Edwards*

Sinclair ZX Spectrum: a Visual Compendium, by Sam Dyer and friends (Bitmap Books)

An attractive book that looks back over the lifetime of the immensely successful ZX Spectrum, which came out in 1982 and provoked an astonishing torrent of games. It has 304 pages, all as bright and colourful as the Spectrum itself. The focus is on graphics and artwork, so the interviews are mostly with artists rather than programmers. The text can be a little bit repetitive, the artists all having been asked the same questions, and giving very similar answers – graph paper and colour clash come up a lot. The company profiles are more interesting, but only five are covered: Ultimate, Beyond, Durell, Odin and Vortex. But as shown by the designer not the writer being identified as the author in the copyright notice, this is a book about the pictures, and they are great, lot of double page spreads of games that still look good today. I regret not having properly played games like *Heavy on*

the Magick, Fairlight and *Tau Ceti*. There are also
several nice pieces of painted artwork by the brilliant
Crash cover artist Oliver Frey. Sadly, nothing appears
from my absolute favourite Spectrum games, the
Gollup brothers' *Rebelstar, Chaos* and *Laser Squad*,
though there's a loading screen from their *Lords of
Chaos*. One surprise was seeing games we had at home
that none of my friends had ever heard of, like *3D
Tanx, Wheelie* and *Harrier Attack!* Another was
realising how few of these games we actually bought,
an initial C90 and C60 from a work friend of my dad
giving me the trading power to build up a massive
library of cassette copies. Tut, tut, young me! A third
surprise was to see on the copyright page that the
Sinclair name and brand is now owned by BSkyB –
can't imagine why they wanted it! Overall, it's a very
expensive book, so not one for casual fans. There are
cheaper retro bookazines to be found in WH Smiths.
But it's very lovely to look at, and my money, at least,
was well spent on it. *Stephen Theaker* ★★★☆☆

A Slip Under the Microscope, by H.G. Wells (Penguin Classics)

The precise definition of science fiction has always
been a matter for debate, the simplest answer being
the stuff H.G. Wells wrote about. With books like *The
Time Machine* (time travel), *The First Men in the Moon*
(space travel), *The War of the Worlds* (alien invasion),
The Shape of Things to Come (future history), *The
Invisible Man* (experimentation on oneself) and *The
Island of Doctor Moreau* (experimentation on others)
he staked out the territory of a genre that still thrives,
still finds new places to go, almost seventy years after
his death. This fifty-five page Penguin Little Black
Classic contains two of his short stories which don't
quite fit that narrative. The title story, "A Slip Under

the Microscope" is science fiction of the *other* kind, a story about science, where a driven young student, labouring under the pressure of being a working class boy at the College of Science, where pupils on scholarships are not even invited to sit down when meeting their tutors, makes a terrible mistake during an examination. The other story, "The Door in the Wall", is more fantastical, about a government minister who longs for the secret garden he found as a child, the magical entrance to which only ever presents itself again when he has not the time to enter it. Both stories are very, very good. The first couple of Little Black Classics I read – *As Kingfishers Catch Fire* by Gerard Manley Hopkins and *Aphorisms on Love and Hate* by Friedrich Nietzsche – were dreadful, but it's clear I judged the series too soon. *Stephen Theaker*
★★★★☆

Stoker's Manuscript, by Royce Prouty (G.P. Putnam's Sons)

Neither fading nor impaling into insignificance.

There are numerous ways to kill a vampire; somewhat fewer to keep him dead. Many a blood-curdling tale has been told. But the modern brow frowns upon capital punishment, so nowadays we prefer neutering (in the sense of making something ineffective). We strap vampires to the operating table and infuse them with a ghastly blend of garlic sauce and teenage hormones. We turn them into that which they most despise.

Throughout history, humankind has taken refuge in dark humour, chuckling grimly where otherwise we might have succumbed to fear. But comedy is not to blame for disempowering the vampire. Programmes like *Count Duckula* – spoofs within genre – were never going to have that effect. Laughter plays its part, yes, but the true weapon has been love: we have pulled vampires unto our collective bosom, discarding our crucifixes so as to subsume them within society's warm embrace.

Buffy the Vampire Slayer brought vampires into the trialled and tribulated domain of teenage life. It used their dark renown as currency against which to stake kick-ass girl power. Buffy's rise brought with it inflation, to the point where individual vampires became virtually worthless. You couldn't give them away. The exception was Angel, but only because he was Buffy's love interest: dark, broody and... good. To survive, it was no longer sufficient for vampires to steer clear of daylight, wooden stakes and razor-sharp chin-up bars. They had to renounce their very identity. They had to reinvent themselves.

The Twilight Saga brought this process to its wretched conclusion, firmly establishing vampires as mysterious, hunky, angst-ridden and easily besotted. Where once they were fearsome and otherworldly, now they manifested as mysterious but desirable; where formerly a different species altogether, now they were no different from any other lugubrious teen: living apart from the rest of the world, self-absorbed and misunderstood. They had issues.

Vampires, in short, became just like anybody else. To use the word pejoratively, they entered the mainstream. Gone was the unspeakable predator; the physically superior, morally bereft killer; the legend and lore; the monster hiding behind a facade of ancient nobility. No longer was there a sense of darkness; no terrible secret underpinning our fear of the unknown. These days, vampires are creatures of the *every*day. There is nothing foreign (let alone alien) about them; nothing out of the ordinary in the hungering urges and bloody depravations that once constituted a force beyond reckoning. The vampire, in

flaccid truth, was taken out of Transylvania, and so too
was Transylvania taken out of the vampire.

In both cases, Royce Prouty has endeavoured to put
it back.

Stoker's Manuscript (Prouty's debut novel) is
centred around the original, unpublished prelude and
concluding section of Bram Stoker's *Dracula*. These
documents are to be auctioned, and antiquarian expert
Joseph Barkeley is engaged to verify their authenticity
and deliver them to an anonymous buyer in Romania.
Having returned thus to his homeland, Barkeley – an
orphan of Romania's communist regime under Nicolae
Ceauçescy – finds that the excised chapters have a
significance far beyond their literary worth... and not
just to the reclusive buyer who resides deep within
Bran Castle.

Perhaps the most satisfying feature of Prouty's
writing is the realism – seemingly innate – with which
he grounds his story. There is a veracity to his
characters, an immediacy to the setting, which
together echo the literature of bygone days in hinting
at fictionalised autobiography. Joseph Barkeley could
be a real person, as could his brother or indeed any of
the humans portrayed. Where popular fiction would
have them splatter the screen or ink-smudge the
written narrative with their motivations, instead these
remain unobtrusive, the players sure-footed in gracing
the pages of Prouty's book. Romania itself is brought
to life with a perspective that makes it eminently
believable, both as a country in the throes of hardship
and as the dark spawning ground of those undead
creatures of legend.

Stoker's Manuscript is a work of supernatural horror,
but it is steeped in history and far from whimsical. The
unreal elements seem disconcertingly plausible. The
horror, though sparse, is all the more gruesome for the
matter-of-fact way in which it is depicted. No aspect is

played up merely to shock the reader; rather, the scenario is allowed simply to unfold, *intrinsically* horrific. The vampires, when they appear, lay claim to absolute dominion. The humans remain helpless; forsaken. Both sanity and sanctity are drawn in to be consumed.

Vampires, before we saw fit to humanise them, had the power to drain us not only of lifeblood but also of spirit, merely through dint of their existence. Occasionally we still tap into the fundamentally chilling dichotomy between them as predator and us as prey – *Blade*, for instance, before it impaled its own premise upon two splintered sequels – but for the most part we seem now to invite vampires into our homes and hearts, the nature of Dracula's progeny becoming just one more trendy accessorising of our own human traits.

Royce Prouty, thankfully, makes no such concession; and where the mainstream would have us be enthralled by a boy crying wolf ever more loudly, ever less plausibly, *Stoker's Manuscript* instead leaves the warning unuttered. Whatever secrets lay buried within Stoker's original manuscript, we don't need to be told that we disinter them at our peril. Yet, in Prouty's world – looming more genuine than many a reality we fashion around ourselves – the *vampyres* of old remain a force to be reckoned with. Restored of both pride and place, they are more truthful to Stoker's original than just about anything that has arisen in the hundred-odd years intervening. Prouty may not be long in the tooth as a novelist, but evidence suggests he might well prove long-lived. *Jacob Edwards*

Tales of the Marvellous and News of the Strange, translated by Malcolm C. Lyons (Penguin Classics)

This is a collection of medieval Arabian fantasy, or at least half of it, the other half being lost to the sands of time. Malcolm C. Lyons provides a new translation, rendering the book rather more readable than the excellent and informative (but spoiler-heavy – read it after the rest of the book) introduction by Robert Irwin suggests the original to be. On Goodreads a potential reader has asked whether the book is suitable for children, and the answer is most definitely no. Grimdark a thousand years before George R.R. Martin or Joe Abercrombie, this is brutal, horrible and cruel, stories of terrible people doing awful things in a world ruled by capricious and sentimental tyrants. Racists, rapists and murderers, these characters lie, cheat and steal their way to happy endings, often saved by a last-minute religious conversion or appeal to a deity. That the stories are about such awful people wouldn't be so jarring if it weren't for the religiosity of it all. Irwin cautions against "the enormous condescension of posterity", quoting E.P. Thompson, and that's a fair point, but it's hard to really enjoy stories in which slavery and sexual aggression are so positively portrayed. For example, in "The Story of Sakhr and Al-Khansa' and of Miqdam and Haifa'", Sakhr sneaks into a girl's tent and draws his sword, saying "if you utter a word I shall make you into a lesson to be talked of amongst all peoples breaking your joints and your bones". The girl "saw that he was handsome as well as eloquent; she weakened and looked down bashfully as he got into bed with her". That's fairly typical, and that story gets worse. The book is also quite repetitive, with everyone who is half-decent to look at being described as like the moon, Indian swords all over the place, people hitting themselves in the face all the time, and every man being "delighted" to discover that his copulative partners are still virgins. (In one case, that's even though they slept together earlier in the story.) That's not to say there's nothing to enjoy here. Though women are generally shown in a terrible light and

PENGUIN CLASSICS

Tales of the Marvellous and
News of the Strange

A MEDIEVAL ARAB FANTASY COLLECTION

treated horribly – for example, a king is told the story
of 'Arus al-'Ara'is to make him glad his daughter died!
– several are shown to live independently and drink
wine very happily. It was surprising to see an
acknowledgment of the existence of gays and lesbians,
even if it was to discourage such romances, and in the
story of the Foundling and Harun al-Rashid there are
heavy hints of male romance. "No one is going to rub
him down except me," says the executioner Masrur in a
bath-house. The story of Miqdad and Mayasa shows
the former killing enemies like a supercharged Conan
the Barbarian and the desert being rolled up for the
latter. In the story of Julnar of the Sea a king says of a
gorgeous woman, "Praise be to God, Who created you
from a vile drop in a secure place!" A nice way of
putting it. The story of Abu Disa is amusing: a
browbeaten weaver is pushed into posing as an
astrologer, and through various turns of fortune makes
a series of astonishing and lucrative predictions. The
story of Sa'id Son of Hatim al-Bahili is a fascinatingly
curious attempt to retcon the Bible. Overall, though, I
found the book such a struggle to get through that I
wouldn't recommend it on its own merits as a
collection of stories; they're just not very good; but as a
curiosity, as a glimpse into the storytelling of the past,
as a translation and as a historical artefact it may find
appreciative readers. *Stephen Theaker* ★★★☆☆

Wailing Ghosts, by Pu Songling (Penguin Classics)

Translated by John Minford, these are fourteen very
short fantasy stories and tall tales, written by a
Chinese author who lived from 1640 to 1715. They are
set in a world of fox spirits, demons and red-headed
monsters. The book doesn't explain its humanoid
foxes, but they seem to be like those in *The Heavenly
Fox* by Richard Parks, where foxes who lived to the age

of fifty could assume human form, and those who lived to a thousand became immortal. Because the stories are so short, it's difficult to say much about them without giving away the entire plot, but the highlights include "King of the Nine Mountains", about a man who rents his back garden out to a party of a thousand fox spirits and promptly betrays them, and "Butterfly", where a syphilitic horny teenager, Luo Zifu, "breaks out in suppurating sores, which left stains on the bedding" and is thus driven out, eventually to find happiness with Butterfly, a supernatural lady who lives a grotto. He blows it, of course. Other stories include "The Monster in the Buckwheat", "Scorched Moth the Taoist", "The Giant Turtle" and "A Fatal Joke", which is barely a page long but features the book's most horrible image. When a book this good costs 80p, you'd be daft not to buy it. *Stephen Theaker* ★★★★☆

Comics

Aldebaran, tome 1: La Catastrophe, by Leo (Dargaud)

Contact with Earth was lost over a hundred years ago, soon after it was hit by an economic crisis, though life isn't too bad on the planet known as Aldebaran. A religious order rules, but their influence is barely felt in Kim's little village on the coast, where the beach is endless and the ocean the sweetest blue. She dreams of getting back in touch with Earth. Marc, a boy who fancies her big sister, works as a fisherman; his dream is to go to the big city. The fishermen find some odd corpses in the water, monsters driven up from the seabed, and a stranger arrives with dire warnings of a disaster to come. No one believes him and he leaves, before a journalist turns up, hot on his trail – Marc takes her after him, and they begin to see some really weird stuff. And maybe it's a good thing he isn't at the village right now...This is the first of five French albums collected in *Aldebaran: L'Integrale*, recently reprinted. It's a gorgeous book, inside and out, and it feels like this first volume barely skims the surface of this strange and beautiful world. Leo's artwork is rather like a slightly stiffer Steve Dillon, his creatures as weird as Miyazaki's. An English translation is available, but it's possible to order the French version through UK Amazon too, if you fancy dusting off your GCSE French. *Stephen Theaker* ★★★★☆

All-Star Section Eight, by Garth Ennis and John McCrea (DC Comics)

A six-issue spin-off from *Hitman* (the comic not the game) which was itself a spin-off from *The Demon*. Tommy Monaghan, the hitman with x-ray vision and a heart of gold, was introduced in the latter during one of DC's dafter crossovers (invading aliens whose attacks gave some people superpowers). He once tried out for the JLA, but the funniest parts of his comic were usually when he ran into alcoholic Sixpack and his band of hopeless heroes, Section Eight, including characters like the Defenestrator, Dogwelder and the pervert Bueno Excellente. Here, at last, they get their own comic, or at least the survivors do, as Sixpack tries to get the team back together. After adding The Grapplah, the demon bartender Baytor, Powertool, Guts and a new Dogwelder (who found the previous guy's outfit in a junk shop), he gets up to seven members, and then tries to persuade the stars of the (New 52) DC universe to fill the last slot. The Martian Manhunter, Wonder Woman and Superman all show up; none seem likely to take the bait. It's funny and

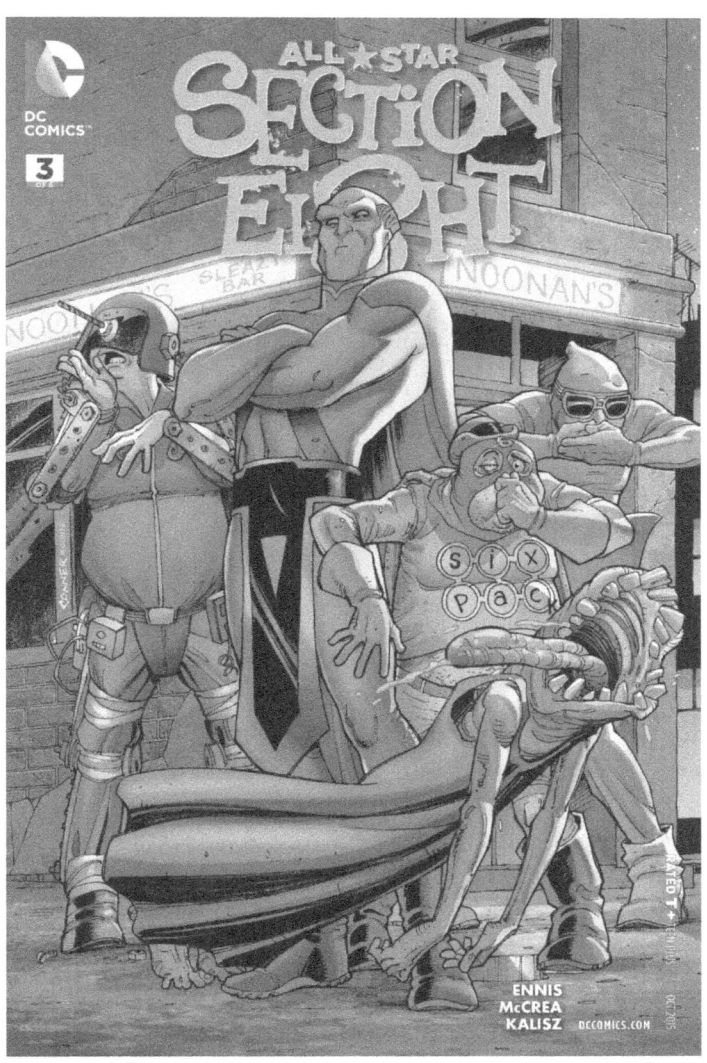

gross, Sixpack's snot, drool and wee depicted in repulsive detail, but also surprisingly moving, by the end reminding me of the classic Doctor Who strip by Scott Gray and Martin Geraghty, "The Land of Happy Endings". Super-heroes may be dumb, but as Garth Ennis writes here, "As dreams go... Well. I suppose you could do worse." This mini-series may not mean very much to people who didn't love *The Demon* or *Hitman*, but it's a must-read for those who did. *Stephen Theaker* ★★★★☆

Atomic Robo, Vol. 7: The Flying She-Devils of the Pacific, by Brian Clevinger and Scott Wegener (Tesladyne)

Atomic Robo is a cool guy created by Nikolai Tesla, who he calls his dad. He is atomic-powered, generally good-natured, and likes a fight. He's strong, wry, almost indestructible, and each graphic novel (or mini-series, in their original publication) takes us to a different period of his life, with different friends and colleagues, previous highlights including battles with giant Nazi robots and cthulhoid monsters. If that sounds a lot like *Hellboy*, that's because it is a lot like *Hellboy* – but with blue skies and daylight. Book seven begins with him flying an experimental plane in 1952, and under attack by weird little flying tanks. Not having any weapons and badly outnumbered, he gets shot down and would be destroyed were it not for a squadron of rocket-women. They kept fighting in the Pacific rather than going home to countries where they'd have to hang up their bomber jackets, their enemies mostly mercenaries, but now there's a bigger threat, and they're going to need Atomic Robo's help to stop it. The previous six *Atomic Robo* books were all very good, and given that this is once again from the same writer and artist it isn't a surprise that this is too. A few panels left me puzzling a little over what was going on, but when I dawdled it was more often to take it all in. The rectangular panels make it ideal for reading on a tablet. Reading one one Atomic Robo book always makes me want to read all of them again. The only sad thing is that the skipping about in time

means we're not likely to meet the she-devils again for a while, a shame because they're rather brilliant.
Stephen Theaker ★★★★☆

Chobits Omnibus, Vol. 1, by CLAMP (Dark Horse)

Hideki is a college kid who is trying to get into Tokyo university, and he doesn't have a lot of money. He certainly can't afford a persocom, a human-shaped computer, so it seems like a stroke of luck when he finds one that's apparently been thrown out with the trash. She seems to be in good condition, and is, incidentally, very pretty, though Hideki is more focused on spreadsheets, word processing and household accounting (by all of which he means pornography). As he carries her off, a disk falls out, and maybe this is why she has no memories, and not even an operating system. He names her Chi, because at first that's all she says. She's a blank slate for Hideki's lessons, and since he's a buffoon that doesn't go well; she ends up unwittingly working for a short spell at a strip club. As the endless pages fly by, she seems to develop feelings for him, while he does for her, even as he is told by himself and others that she's a machine and such feelings are a waste. Would he be better off spending his time with Yumi Omura, a peppy student with a crush on him? Then there's Takako Shimizu, a college tutor who turns up at his house for an impromptu sleepover, and Chitose Hibiya, his beautiful landlady, who is keeping a couple of big secrets, and knows a few about Chi, who might be one of the fabled Chobits, persocoms that can learn for themselves. Although this manga translation is presented in the now-traditional right-to-left format, the limited amount of dialogue per page stops it from being too confusing to read. The backgrounds are plain, as little art as possible being used to fill each page – the printing costs that have shaped US comics so much were presumably less of an issue as comics developed in Japan. I've never before read a book so long in which so little happens. It only took a couple of hours to read, despite being 740pp long. (This explains those fifteen-year-old Goodreads users with thousands of books read.) The "sexy" elements of it tend to be a bit gross, especially in retrospect after we're told late in the book the apparent age of Chi's physical body. It has some interesting ideas about how easily humans would switch their affections to such androids, sidestepping the problems and complexities of human romance. It's undemanding, occasionally amusing, a bit pompous, and it kept me busy while I drank a cup of tea; if volume two comes up in a sale I might possibly buy it, but otherwise I'd be happy to leave Hideki to perv over his personal computer in private. *Stephen Theaker* ★★★☆☆

Doctor Who Comic #7, by Robbie Morrison, Brian Williamson and chums (Titan Comics)

A wonderfully substantial publication that collects four issues of the ongoing US format comics, one each from the twelfth and tenth Doctors' comics, and two from the eleventh Doctor's title. In "The Fractures, Part 2", by Robbie Morrison and Brian Williamson, the twelfth Doctor and Clara are trying to help a UNIT scientist from another dimension. His wife and daughters died in a car crash, and they live on here, but when he crossed the void between dimensions he attracted the attention of the Fractures. Visually it's not up to the standards of the strips that appear in *Doctor Who Magazine*, but it's enjoyable enough. The eleventh Doctor's story "The Eternal Dogfight" (complete in this issue), by Rob Williams, Al Ewing and Warren Pleece, sees him accompanied by three new companions: a shape-changing alien, a depressed assistant librarian, and a chubby David Bowie type. An everlasting dogfight between two fleets of alien combatants has drifted into Earth's vicinity, and if the

Doctor and friends can't bring it to an end there could be eight billion civilian casualties. All very entertaining, in thanks part to the intrigue of each new companion's ongoing story, and the jolly artwork. It reminded me of the early Tom Baker strips in *Doctor Who Weekly*. The tenth Doctor is also joined by a new companion – Gabby, an American from New York – for his story, "The Weeping Angels of Mons, Part 2", by Robbie Morrison and Daniel Indro. The statuesque monsters of the title are snatching soldiers from the trenches of World War I. It's an interesting story, and the artwork (including the colouring by Slamet Mujiono) suits it perfectly, the expressions of the angels being as alarming as one would hope never to see. I liked each individual story, but it's the cumulative effect of reading almost a hundred pages of new Doctor Who comics that makes it so rewarding. I subscribed before getting even halfway through it. *Stephen Theaker* ★★★★☆

Showcase Presents Ambush Bug, by Keith Giffen, Robert Loren Fleming and friends (DC Comics)

A 488pp black and white collection of comics, mostly from the mid-eighties. The bulk of it comes from two mini-series, *Ambush Bug* (1985) and *Son of Ambush Bug* (1986), plus a couple of specials, his story from *Secret Origins*, and earlier guest appearances in Superman titles. Ambush Bug is the costumed identity of Irwin Schwab, who knows he's in a comic, talks to his writers and artists, and doesn't necessarily go from one page to the next in the usually accepted order. His best friend and adopted child is Cheeks the Toy Wonder, a stuffed toy, and his greatest foes are the Interferer, who messes with comics continuity because he can, and Argh-Yle, a sock from a spaceship that got squashed by a radioactive space-spider, came to life and became a supervillain, and now tries to conquer the world with living socks from a chest of drawers (The Bureau) orbiting the planet. Reading that back, it's hard to understand why I didn't like it very much. It sounds like a lot of fun, and Deadpool has had great success with a similar shtick. But I laughed only three or four times in the course of all these pages (the best being when Keith Giffen's famous nine-panel layouts are said to be inspired by *Celebrity Squares*). Maybe it's the lack of colour in this edition, which makes all the busy, busy pages a bit hard to read, or that there's so much frantically packed in, which might have worked better taken in single issue doses. A lot of the humour is aimed at comics and controversies in the field from the mid-eighties, and though I've read enough of those to get the gist, I didn't find them funny. Maybe the clue is in the panel five pages from the end where Ambush Bug declares "I *hate* British humour". Though I do appreciate the cleverness there of spelling it with a U. *Stephen Theaker* ★★☆☆☆

The Technopriests, Vol. 1: Techno Pre-School, by Alexandro Jodorowsky, Zoran Janjetov and Fred Beltran (Humanoids)

Albino the Supreme Technopriest is on a spaceship with five hundred thousand of his brethren, travelling from one galaxy to another, where they hope to start a new society, where healthy relationships will count for more than scientific advances. It's the perfect time to kick back and think over his eventful life to date: this first book in the series begins with the horrific events that led to his mother's pregnancy. Understandably consumed by bitterness, she vows revenge on Ulritch the Red and his fellow pirates. Young Albino is left to feed at the breast of a guanodont, and grows up working in his mother's cheese factory, with only

ALEXANDRO JODOROWSKY
ZORAN JANJETOV & FRED BELTRAN
THE TECHNOPRIESTS
#1: TECHNO PRE-SCHOOL

HUMANOÏDS

computer games and little Tinigrifi, a talking
(android?) bunny, to keep him sane. Eventually she
arranges for him to attend the Technopriest training
school of Don Mossimo, where his cleverness attracts
the attention of a Techno-Bishop, while she amasses
enough money to hire the mercenaries she needs for
her revenge. The artwork by Janjotov and the
colouring by Beltran are tremendous throughout,
detailed and fascinating, only let down by some jarring

computer graphics used to illustrate scenes of virtua-walking in cyberspace. This boy lives in a weird world full of peculiar people, not least his own family, and that side of it was good, but there's an awful lot of sexual violence, right at the heart of the story, and the "Tee hee" from Tinigrifi that follows one event feels misjudged, to say the least. As well as individual digital volumes, the entire series is available in a single hardback omnibus. *Stephen Theaker* ★★★☆☆

Y: The Last Man, Vol. 1: Unmanned, by Brian K. Vaughan, Pia Guerra and José Marzán, Jr (Vertigo)

Every man and boy in the world starts throwing up blood and drops down dead, all at the same time. Is it because the Amulet of Helene has been taken out of Jordan, bringing on an ancient prophecy of catastrophe? Or because Doctor Mann gave birth to her own clone? Or because Yorick Brown proposed to his best friend with a ring he bought in a magic shop for half the money he had? The only man who might find out is Yorick himself, because he's the only man to survive (at least so far as we know from this book). All the male non-humans died too, except for his capuchin monkey Ampersand. Others might have seen the resulting situation as a golden opportunity for a healthy young man, but not Yorick, he's in love with Beth, and she's in Australia, so like James Garner in *Support Your Local Sheriff* that's where he's heading, whatever else distracts him in the meantime. It's a dangerous world for a man, where anyone he meets could want to sell, kill or enslave him, but his mother asks him to go with the awesome Agent 355 to find Dr Mann – together they might be the best hope for the world, especially if they can figure out why Yorick survived. This is an excellent book. It has a great premise, and this volume begins to explore the

ramifications of that premise in fascinating ways. For example, Yorick's mother is a representative in Congress, and because the Democrats have more female representatives there than the Republican, they become a majority when the men die. Pia Guerra and José Marzán, Jr's art is perfect, reminiscent in its clarity and structure of Steve Dillon's work on *Preacher* for the same publisher, but with character all of its own. The book's weakest link is probably Yorick himself, who isn't half as interesting and charismatic as the female characters that surround him. *Stephen Theaker* ★★★★☆

Films

Ant-Man, by Edgar Wright, Joe Cornish and others (Marvel Films)

Scott Lang (played with great charm by Paul Rudd) used to have principles, but he became a cat burglar to expose corporate corruption, and found he was good at it. He's been in prison a while, and after getting out tries to go straight, but it's tough to get or keep a job with his record, and soon he's back with his group of criminal friends (you can't blame him, they're a funny bunch of fellows) and planning a new job. They're going to break into the house of Hank Pym. Yes, that Hank Pym, the original Ant-Man, but here he is older and played by Michael Douglas. (Who has, may I say, left it way too late in his career to change his mind about acting in fantasy films. Just imagine the films he could have got made in his prime.) It's easy to understand why the film-makers decided to skip over Pym, given his unwholesome history in the comics, and especially in *The Ultimates*, such an influence on the Avengers films, but at least they give him a history as Ant-Man – albeit a secret one, as a covert operative. Anyway, one thing leads to another and before you know it Scott is wearing the Ant-Man suit he stole and Hank is training him to use it. It lets him shrink to the size of an ant, and talk to them too. Also helping with the training is Janet van Dyne, Pym's daughter, played by Evangeline Lilly, so good in *Lost* and the Hobbit films, and equally good here. There's a bad guy working on the same technology, who has taken over Pym's company, and he's happy to kill lots of sheep to get it working. Can Scott pull himself together and save the day when he's under more pressure than ever?

It was surprising that this film wasn't worse,

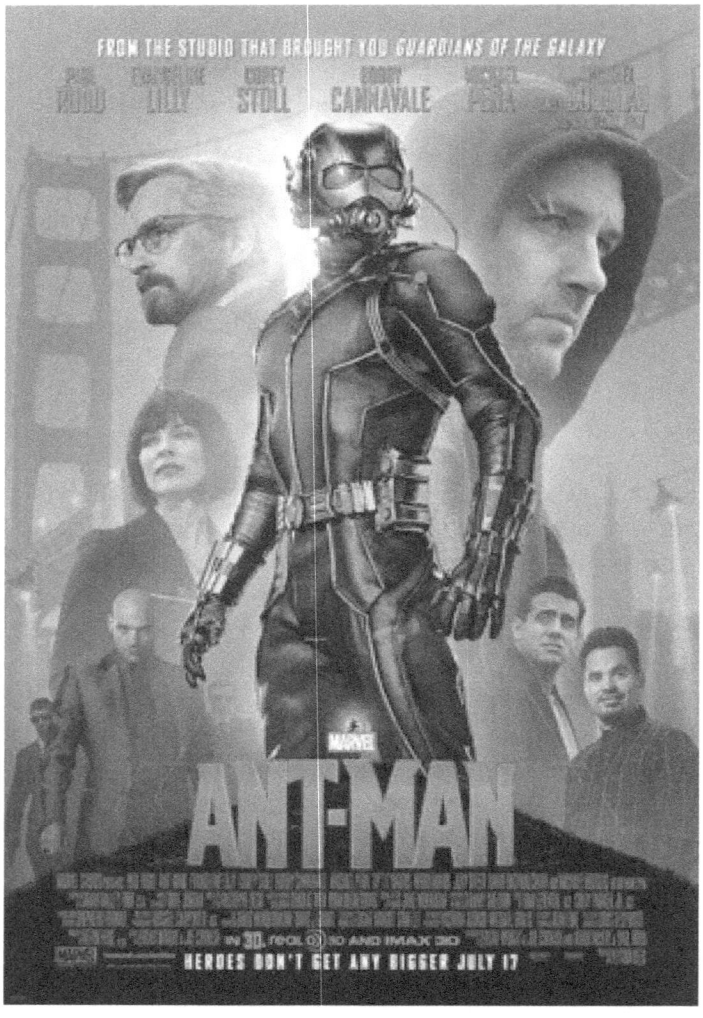

knowing the little bit that we do of the circumstances in which it was made, intended director Edgar Wright leaving the picture after years of development. It's hard not to feel it's the ghost of the film it would have been, though it's clearly very close to what he planned: he and Joe Cornish still get the screenplay credit, his trademark use of music (The Cure, in this case) and edits (a sequence showing how a rumour gets passed around) are still on display, and the scene of Ant-Man fighting two security guards looks exactly like it did in the original proof-of-concept footage shown at San Diego Comic-Con. An interpolated fight with one of the Avengers seems most out of place, both in the film and in Ant-Man's career: there's no way he should have been able to hold his own with an experienced hero yet. (Though I still enjoyed it.) This could have been one of the best of the Marvel movies, but it's not too bad as it is, it's decent enough.

An aside: some reviewers have commented on the misgendering of the ants in the film, with Ant-Man calling them guys and giving his favourite a boy's name. We saw it in France, VOSTF-style, and it was interesting to see that the subtitles changed all that, with Scott shouting for *les filles* and calling his favourite ant Antoinette: a little example of how things can change in translation. *Stephen Theaker* ★★★☆☆

Goosebumps, by Darren Lemke (Columbia Pictures et al.)

Classic Black over-the-top performance saves otherwise ho hum "house next door has a secret" film.

In the 2002 film *Orange County*, Jack Black plays the drug-addled Lance Brumder who, clad only in his briefs, wanders his wealthy parents' home. The role epitomizes the take-it-as-it-comes, let-it-all-hang-out California attitude that Black injects into his characters. The strategy has resulted in everything from chummy teachers that appeal to families (*School of Rock* (2003)) to hell-bent rocker scumbags that appeal to young adults (*Tenacious D in The Pick of Destiny* (2006)).

This time, Black reprises his penchant for

exaggeration as a reclusive and mean-spirited R.L. Stine, the real-life author of the best-selling Goosebumps collection now 62 books strong, in a film of the same name.

True to the Stine canon, the PG-rated film, directed by Rob Letterman, threatens its young protagonists with monsters, but nobody gets seriously hurt. Even a young man pulled through the upper-level window of a gymnasium by a giant praying mantis will later appear in a neck brace.

Though the film foists on the viewer cliché after cliché, Black's overly impassioned performance is enough to keep viewers engaged in this bubblegum horror/adventure version of *Jumanji* (1995).

Monster Mash
After the loss of his father, Zach and his mother move from New York City to the quiet suburb of Madison, Delaware. Here Zach meets love interest Hannah and her over-protective father (Black). "You see that fence? Stay on your side of it."

When Zach believes Hannah's father may be violent, he enlists new high school acquaintance and bumbling sidekick Champ (short for Champion) to help get to the bottom of it. The duo unwittingly unleash a monster trapped in one of Stine's manuscripts. This incident kicks off the action that drives the rest of the story.

The remainder of the film isn't hard to predict. More monsters escape from their textual prisons. Stine and the kids try to stop a growing monster posse without being eaten, crushed, stabbed, clawed, etc. Meanwhile, Stine's true intentions and vulnerabilities are revealed. The film culminates in a high school dance turned monster mash in a frenzy comparable to (though not quite as entertaining as) that in *Pixels* (2015).

Goosebumps also offers a cameo by the real author. Jack Black's high school English teacher version of Stine introduces the true Stine as the drama teacher, Mr Black.

The Black Side of Goosebumps
Without Black, *Goosebumps* would have been a dull rehash of the monsters and themes that we've seen a thousand times. Black's performance is most enjoyable in the beginning: the camera zooms in on his bulldog-like face, which contrasts with the fifties-style thick-lensed glasses and the oiled hair. The thin-lipped mouth contortions and the affected super-professorial accent round out the impression.

Even when a gang of creepily animated porcelain gnomes attacks the heroes, Black's cartoonish physicality entertains.

Though not much beyond Black tickles the funny bone in *Goosebumps*, it does have its moments, such as when Champ points out to Zach the massive scratch marks in a wall. I'm paraphrasing: "Did you see these scratch marks?" Zach's sarcastic response: "No. I didn't."

The lead book-born bad guy is a dummy named Slappy, voiced by Black. Though Black's voiceover is well-played, Slappy's one-liners would make Freddy Krueger and the Crypt Keeper cringe. Moreover, despite his girlish screams, Champ's antics grow a bit irritating. Nevertheless, I've seen excerpts of the child-directed television shows that my nieces watch and I've been tempted to knock myself out due to the painfully exuberant (and unfunny) performances of those show's stars. Champ is consistent.

Though *Goosebumps* does not achieve the same level of humour and enduring charm as *School of Rock*, Black's faulted character again grows from the younger players and vice-versa.

Jack Black brings a Bill Murray mentality to his projects. It's as if they're nudging the viewer and saying, "Hey, if you don't take this film too seriously, then I won't take this role too seriously. And we'll have a good time together." In *Goosebumps*, we do. *Douglas J. Ogurek* ★★★★☆

The Green Inferno, by Eli Roth and Guillermo Amoedo (Worldview Entertainment et al.)

Eli Roth devises perfect film for family movie night or corporate team building event... if your house or office happens to be in hell.

It was literary giant Anton Chekhov, I believe, who said, "If you show in the first act images of female genital mutilation (FGM) during a university lecture, in the second or third act you absolutely must move toward the cutting." Or was that guns he was talking about?

FGM is a real-world atrocity that splatter master Eli Roth holds over the victims (and audience) in *The Green Inferno*, a limb-hacking, skin-slicing tale of good intentions turned cannibalistic nightmare.

With *The Green Inferno*, Roth takes to new lows the depravity he so adroitly captured in *Hostel* (2005) and *Hostel: Part II* (2007). Once again, he traps young adults far away from home in a horrific environment occupied by depraved individuals, but this time, the collective antagonist shifts from psychotic plutocrats in a ravaged Slovakian cityscape to cold-blooded cannibals in a Peruvian rainforest.

A group of university activists travels to the Amazon with hopes of stopping developers from killing off a remote tribe and destroying its land. Protagonist Justine, daughter of a United Nations lawyer, gets pressured into going by Alejandro, the group's snarky leader. The plane goes down, the group gets caged, and then the barbarity begins.

A Rocky Start Redeemed
The film's beginning, which builds up to Justine's decision to join the group, is dull and at times amateurish. Justine and her sickly-looking, smug roommate Kaycee wander around campus and engage in mindless chatter. Perhaps this was Roth's attempt to show average kids in College Town, USA. Regardless, it took too long to get the characters into the enemy's clutches.

However, once the viewer experiences these savages (in every sense of the word), the film's early shortcomings can be forgiven. Eli Roth, who so enthusiastically bashed in the head of a Nazi officer as Sgt. Donny Donowitz in *Inglorious Basterds* (2009), is not about characters. Roth is about creating worlds where violence, gore, and victimization reign supreme. *The Green Inferno* exceeds expectations on all accounts.

The Mob and the Matriarch
One of the film's key strengths is the way it conveys the tribe's maliciousness, ranging from the overall portrayal of the group to the behaviour of twisted individuals. The scene during which the tribe ushers the students to a cage exemplifies the former. The natives sway and chant and paw at their terrified prisoners. With their red body paint, the tribe members seem to shed their humanity and coagulate into a many-tentacled Lovecraftian monstrosity. The shifting, chaotic nature of Roth's filming immerses the viewer in the danger.

Nobody embodies the tribe's malice more than its wrinkled matriarch, whose piercings, yellow face paint, and milky eye suggest the literary lovechild of Ray Bradbury and Edgar Allen Poe. She sizes up her captives as she limps predatorily across the screen. She oozes potential violence as she uses a claw to examine their hair, faces, and (in the case of females) nether regions with the patience of a connoisseur at a delicatessen.

Raise the Bar for Bad
Films often show the chief antagonist commit a

particularly heinous initial act to show just how bad
he or she is. In the case of *The Green Inferno*, it's the
matriarch who fulfils this role, and in so doing,
achieves the height of gore with a genuine
showstopper of slaughter.

The reader may recall the wood chipper scene that
earned *Fargo*'s (1996) Gaear Grimsrud a reputation for
dispassionate brutality. The tribal matriarch, however,
injects a Broadway-worthy flamboyance to her key
scene, which makes *Fargo* look like Sesame Street.
That scene kicks off what quickly becomes a
smorgasbord of psychological terror (who's going to be
next?) and sumptuously over-the-top gore (e.g.
children trying on flaps of skin as if at a fashion store).

The Green Inferno offers a lawless world where good
isn't necessarily rewarded, nor bad punished. Suffering
is random, based on the whim of an antagonist whose
motives are impossible to comprehend. The film raises
some questions on benevolence versus self-
preservation, and on the treacherousness of humans
in contrast to the necessities of animals.

Kudos to Eli Roth for serving up a new classic in
goreography and for continuing to slice apart
Hollywood conventions. *Douglas J. Ogurek* ★★★★★

**The Hunger Games: Mockingjay, Part 2, by Peter
Craig and Danny Strong (Lionsgate etc)**

Inspirational series closes with a fizzle.

In *Mockingjay – Part 2*, the fourth and final
installment of the hitherto superb *The Hunger Games*
series, something slips. The viewer feels disconnected
from the characters. Their dialogue sounds contrived
and melodramatic. The emotional investment in the
fate of Panem seems tempered. When characters flee
from life-threatening dangers, they appear to jog
rather than sprint.

The primary suspect for this tepid conclusion is the decision to split the final episode in Suzanne Collins's trilogy of novels into two films (both directed by Francis Lawrence). It's not impossible to do this successfully: the *Twilight* dynasty did it with *Breaking Dawn Parts 1* and *2*, and Peter Jackson segmented Tolkien's novel *The Hobbit* into three phenomenal films.

Though *Mockingjay – Part 1* (2014) held its own as a tense segue to a finale, *Part 2* doesn't follow through: too much time holed up in dark rooms watching televised updates. Too much chatter among humdrum characters. Too much filler and not enough substance.

Most of *Mockingjay – Part 2* details protagonist Katniss Everdeen (Jennifer Lawrence) and a small unit journeying on foot through a mostly abandoned Capitol. The group hangs back from the front line so its videographers can document Katniss, revered among rebels as the Mockingjay... the embodiment of their revolution. Katniss plays along with this charade so that she can pursue her ultimate goal of assassinating President Snow (Donald Sutherland), the Capitol's Machiavellian leader.

On their way, the group must contend with "pods" that unleash deadly weapons and with the Capitol's Stormtrooper-like Peacekeepers. Unfortunately, these challenges are far too scarce.

Katniss travels with competing love interests Gale Hawthorne (Liam Hemsworth) and Peeta Mellark (Josh Hutcherson), but the intensity of their rivalry pales in comparison to that of, for instance, *Twilight*'s Jacob Black and Edward Cullen. Gale has all the personality of a robot, and Peeta's struggle to keep himself from offing Katniss – he's been brainwashed by the Capitol – grows tedious. One finds oneself saying, "Ah get over it, already!"

In my review of *The Hunger Games: Catching Fire*

(2013), I stated the film may have achieved the rare distinction of outshining the book. This time around, the book has reclaimed its title.

Bright Spots
Mockingjay – Part 2 certainly was not a total failure. A couple of action sequences come to mind: one in which the group faces an oil flood in an enclosed space while Peeta goes cuckoo, and another in which Katniss and company engage in an underground battle with "muttations" (aka "mutts") with no eyes and massive teeth.

The film's climax manages to resurface the vibe of its predecessors. Despite thousands of spectators, drumbeats make the only sound as Katniss promenades toward an action that will shock Panem. It's a sharp contrast to the cheering and screaming that accompanied her on the same walk in previous episodes.

The talents of the film's true stars carry over. It's a pleasure to watch Julianne Moore as Alma Coin, the opportunistic and manipulative leader of the rebel army. She sees Katniss as a tool to aid her rise to power and eventual usurpation of President Snow. But just how far will Coin, with her lizard-like eyes, take her Macbethian ambition?

Another treat is Coin's constantly smirking co-conspirator, the Gamemaker and public perception guru Plutarch Heavensby, played by Philip Seymour Hoffman. Rarely is a know-it-all so likable.

With President Snow, Donald Sutherland offers a nuanced supervillain who stays true to his character. Whether he's sipping liqueur amid his panderers or facing an imminent threat, Snow simultaneously conveys repulsion toward and admiration for his chief adversary Katniss Everdeen.

In the film's most moving scene, Jennifer Lawrence

once again proves her Oscar worthiness as she mourns the loss of a loved one. It's a rage- and grief-fuelled release that brings together all the injustice and pain that she's suffered. Brilliant.

Dystopia Denied
During Katniss's earlier Hunger Games exploits, her

mentor Haymitch Abernathy (Woody Harrelson) repeatedly advises her to better relate to her television audience. This autonomous young lady, despite her heroic feats and eventual Mockingjay moniker, has trouble connecting with others. Lovey-dovey Katniss Everdeen is not.

Moreover, the hardships that Katniss endures throughout the series arguably make her less connected, perhaps even cold. This is war, and war leaves lifelong psychological scars.

Considering this, it was hugely disappointing to watch a rainbows and butterflies conclusion that abruptly supplants a dystopian world with that of a fairy tale. It's an insult to the sombre tone that pervades these films and the books. Katniss Everdeen is not a caretaker. Katniss Everdeen is a survivor.
Douglas J. Ogurek ★★★☆☆

Krampus, by Todd Casey, Michael Dougherty and Zach Shields (Legendary Pictures et al.)

Killjoys beware: this holiday horror surprises with positive message, tender moments.

A colleague expressed reservations about Krampus. How could I, he wondered, want to see a horror movie that ostensibly spits in the face of the Christmas holiday spirit?

As it turns out, this individual is way off the mark. Yes, *Krampus* is billed as a horror film. Yes, the demonic title character is, if you'll pardon the expression, the *polar* opposite of Santa Claus. At first glance, *Krampus* seems little more than sprinkling some red and green on the typical B/slasher film in which a savvy monster gradually picks off unlikable or shallow characters.

What a pleasant surprise, therefore, when the film demolishes that expectation by morphing into a warm and, at times, touching commentary on overcoming the burdens that threaten to deflate the Christmas spirit. *Krampus* cautions the viewer to embrace what's most important about the holiday season: family and hope.

Rarely does a film offer the range of experiences that *Krampus* does. Among the gifts it stuffs into our experiential stockings are humour, terror, sadness, triumph, anger, empathy, and appreciation. What more could one ask for?

Whether your fancy is spiked drinks and fireplaces, characters in conflict, or monsters, *Krampus* has something for you. Where else can you find a film in which a massive mystical creature terrifies a teenage girl, a character gets his "ass kicked by a bunch of Christmas cookies", and a presumed insensitive sap offers a heartfelt apology?

Krampus rivets the viewer from its humorous Black Friday opening sequence to its not bleak, though certainly not "happily ever after" conclusion.

A Problem Much Bigger Than a Feisty Squirrel
The film kicks off in *National Lampoon's Christmas Vacation* (1989) fashion: the Engel family (parents Tom and Sarah and kids Beth and Max) welcome to their suburban home the much more eccentric brood of Sarah's sister Linda. Standouts include patriarch Howard (played by David Koechner), a pair of sisters who've been raised like boys, and the hard-drinking, ultra-blunt Aunt Dorothy.

The tension starts the moment the visitors walk through the door, then carries over to an entertaining dinner scene rife with insults, embarrassment, and humour.

The film abruptly darkens when Max gives up his hope on Santa (and, to him, the spirit of the season).

Forget the squirrel that troubles the Griswolds; here
comes Krampus, the horned, cloven-hoofed demon!

In an artful story-within-a-story, Omi Engel, Tom's
German-speaking mother, shares the Krampus legend
accompanied by what a twenty-something creative
professional might call a "sick" computer-generated

comic-like scene. "Krampus came not to reward," says Omi, "but to punish. Not to give, but to take."

Fuelled by Max's hopelessness, Krampus and his minions spend the rest of the film terrorizing (but also bonding) the families.

Beyond Campy

What gives *Krampus* more depth than the typical comedy-horror is a series of tender moments that make you fall in love with the family. It happens between the adult sisters, but even more impressively between the fathers. Tom Engel's attachment to his obviously white collar job has caused some rifts within his family. Conversely, Howard, a toned-down version of Eddie in *Christmas Vacation*, is a shotgun-toting Republican with no qualms about attacking Tom's lack of manliness. When the stakes rise and force these two to put their heads together, we see some genuinely moving scenes.

Many campy horror movies present characters that viewers *want* to get killed. In *Krampus*, the feeling is different. Squabbles are put aside. Weaknesses are admitted. Sacrifices are made. Even characters portrayed as jerks begin to warm our hearts. Suddenly, you don't want them to die.

The Chilling Side

Let's not forget that *Krampus* is, above all, a horror movie. So the question is... does it hold its own as a horror? The answer is a resounding yes. Though the majority of the film's horror falls into the "cute" or "humorous" categories, there are instances of oddity and outright hair-raising spectacle.

Krampus's initial appearance stands as one of the most well-done horror action sequences this viewer has seen in the last couple of years. One character encounters him on a snowy suburban street. The screen only reveals Krampus's hugeness and his horns, but the simultaneous fluidity and power of his movements would strike fear into the heart of anyone.

Moreover, Krampus's minions offer a collection of scenes both funny and chilling. A few come to mind: a kind of fireplace fishing using a cookie as bait, a mysteriously growing collection of creepy-looking snowmen, bastardized elves and reindeer, and an attic scene brimming with *Evil Dead*-like threats.

Watch It

Krampus catches humanity on a precipice. As the holidays approach, will we embrace the spirit of the season? Or will we fall prey to the temptations of materialism and greed?

The leading monster is not totally evil, nor is he willing to give complete exemption to those seeking repentance. Krampus might be all about taking, but the one thing he surely gives is a great moviegoing experience. So... you better watch it. *Douglas J. Ogurek*
★★★★★

Star Wars: The Force Awakens, by Lawrence Kasdan, J.J. Abrams and Michael Arndt (Lucasfilm et al.)

This one lives up to the fever.

An acquaintance of mine arrived at *Star Wars: The Force Awakens* while in the throes of a fever. Director J.J. Abrams had a daunting task: to cut through this individual's nausea, back pain, and somewhat clouded mental capacity. Plus this acquaintance wasn't the brightest lightsaber in the bunch; what kind of guy goes to the theatre sick?

When the film ended, he was still in pain. However, during the two-plus hours of space battles, lightsaber duels, inspiring music, and settings ranging from vast deserts to cramped spaceships, this fellow mostly forgot his condition and instead basked in the tonic powers (my words, not his) of a simple, yet highly entertaining story.

Impelled by my acquaintance's recommendation, I saw the film. Kudos to Mr Abrams!

When it comes to dumbed down one-word summaries of five-star films, there's a big difference between "wow" and "cool". "Wow" describes a consciousness-jarring work that embeds itself in the viewer for life. "Wow" is *Titanic* (1997), *There Will Be Blood* (2007), or, in the case of genre films, *Signs* (2002) or *Paranormal Activity* (2007).

"Cool", on the other hand, provides a more in-the-moment experience. The "cool" film's contents include the latest special effects, stimulating action sequences, and, often, clear distinctions between good and evil.

Star Wars: The Force Awakens undoubtedly falls into the "cool" category. There is nothing extraordinarily new or surprising about this seventh installment in the ultimate sci-fi series, yet it manages to capture the essence that made the prior episodes (apologies to haters of episodes I–III) so enchanting. *The Force Awakens* resurfaces all the things we love most about Star Wars, from TIE fighters and AT-AT walkers to alien bars and stylized scene wipes. And the *Millennium Falcon* is treated with as much reverence as if it were a character. *The Force Awakens* also offers plenty of melodrama; I suppose that's why they call it "space opera".

This film smartly latches onto the craze for crusader-heroines like Katniss Everdeen (*The Hunger Games* series) and Tris Prior (*Divergent* series). This time, it's Rey, played by Daisy Ridley. Unlike her counterparts Everdeen and Prior roaming a dystopian future US, Rey lives on the desert planet of Jakku. Moreover, she isn't encumbered by love interests or prone to teary indecision. Rey, an independent young woman with a difficult (if not very clear) past, scavenges to make her meagre earnings. Her journey begins when she meets BB-8, an R2-D2-like droid and, shortly thereafter, Finn, a Stormtrooper gone rogue.

Both the good guys (the Resistance) and the bad guys (the First Order) want the same thing: to find Luke Skywalker, who has gone into hiding after one of his Jedi Knight trainees went over to the dark side of the Force. The Resistance wants Luke to help revive

the mostly dormant Force and help protect the galaxy, while the Nazi-like First Order wants to destroy Luke and conquer the galaxy.

One of the biggest shortcomings of *The Force Awakens* is the emotional disconnect between characters, which unfortunately transfers to the viewer. (But were we ever that close to these characters?) Also abrasive were some of the post explosion/destruction celebratory colloquialisms. "Did you see that?! Did you see that?!" This is supposed to be "a long time ago in a galaxy far far away", not "today in the United States".

Notable is that the new generation heroes are relatively unknown and retain a quiet, though strong presence consistent with Ewan McGregor's performance as Obi-Wan Kenobi in episodes I–III. Adam Driver excels as Kylo Ren, a Darth Vader wannabe and kind of First Order roving bully who transitions from rage-induced lightsaber tantrums to tense one-on-one conversations. When Kylo Ren is masked, Driver's thin frame and black cloak give him a Grim Reaper-like appearance. When the mask comes off during key scenes, his previous behaviour, doe-eyed expression, and Josh Groban hairstyle add to the mystery of whether Kylo Ren will go berserk or break into "O Holy Night".

So take *The Force Awakens*, in sickness and in health; it will captivate unconditionally. It *is* cool. Definitely cool. *Douglas J. Ogurek* ★★★★★

Star Wars: The Force Awakens, by Lawrence Kasdan, J.J. Abrams and Michael Arndt (Lucasfilm et al.) (take two)

Déjàvooine Sunrise.

Star Wars Episode VII: The Force Awakens (if we may be allowed a scrolling preamble) has been

released with considerable fanfare and after much
anticipation. Like the birth of Prince George, Duke of
Cambridge, its arrival brings together a nation of fans
united in pride, patriotism, hope and nostalgia (and,
be warned, young George, with a bevy of concealed
weapons held at the ready). At last! A renewal of the
franchise that blew up the box office in 1977 and grew
quickly to become – for some people quite literally – a
cinematic religion. But those who queue for midnight
screenings do so with some trepidation. Given the
false dawn of the prequelogy (Episodes I–III), will this
merely be more of the tepid same? How will the new
film tie in with the Expanded Star Wars Universe? Will
the original characters return and stay true to memory
three decades on? Will director J.J. Abrams bring with
him an unconscionable crosspollination from the Star
Trek franchise? In short, will Star Wars survive its
metamorphosis to the post-Lucas era? The story
continues...

If cinemagoers expected or feared change, their first
impressions must have been reassuringly to the
contrary. George Lucas may have been bought out by
Disney but the men and women with mouse ears
made certain to retain John Williams, whose
magniloquent orchestral scores swept audiences away
and complemented so well the epic scope of the
original movies. Star Wars without John Williams
would be like early PC games without MIDI-pop
soundtracks, only louder in the absence. Thankfully,
The Force Awakens features Williams in all his
incomparable pomp and majesty, reprising earlier
themes where appropriate and showcasing new
compositions through which sizzling lifeblood Star
Wars is enabled to soar anew.

Bringing back the (quote) good bits of Star Wars
seems to have been a large part of J.J. Abrams' modus
operandi. This is evident not just in the score but in

his favouring of scale models, location filming and practical effects over the glitzy do-anything wowbagging of CGI. George Lucas is said to have criticised the film's retro tone – something he himself strove to avoid in the prequels, with lamentable consequence – yet by returning to the roots of what made the original trilogy great, Episode VII recaptures the sense of enormousness that Episode IV brought so singularly to the screen. For want of a better word, *The Force Awakens* makes Star Wars feel big again.

A New Hope dazzled in part by way of its originality, so recapturing its spirit would necessarily encompass a certain amount of modernising. This accounts for such curiosities in *The Force Awakens* as the mediaeval-styled light-longsword (verdict out; those handguards look likely to endanger the user) and a buzzing new piece of stormtrooper kit (in essence a riot stick energised for duelling against lightsabers). It also explains why droid favourite R2-D2 is side-lined in favour of the equally inspired BB-8 and why C-3PO is limited to one resplendent cameo. In a similar vein, Chewbacca and his bowcaster are depicted more powerfully, while the formerly disposable stormtroopers are transformed from candy-coated featherweights into genuine enforcers. In this instance, to Abrams' great credit, the spirit of yesteryear's Star Wars has been bolstered by a logic and gravitas *A New Hope* sometimes lacked.

Which brings us to the original cast [**and hereafter, major spoilers**]. Star Wars Episodes IV–VI were carried by relatively unknown actors (supported of course by industry doyens Alec Guinness and Peter Cushing). The main characters thus came without preloaded expectations; nothing to distract viewers from the unfolding story. This decision may have been financially motivated, at least for *A New Hope*, yet when Episodes I–III arrived and went largely in the other direction, the overabundance of acting talent served only to break the illusion and show up the shallowness of the scripts. With J.J. Abrams looking to the past, would *The Force Awakens* dust off Leia, Luke and Han or return instead to a more obscure cast...?

The answer is a little of both, but leaning very much in the right direction. We're given John Boyega as stormtrooper deserter Finn (the naïve Luke figure); Daisy Ridley as self-reliant, tech-savvy scavenger Rey (a combination of Han and Leia); and Adam Driver as partially trained dark side Force warrior Kylo Ren (part Luke, part Vader wannabe). None of these are without standing in the industry, but they aren't name actors. Unlike prequelogy stars Liam Neeson, Ewan McGregor, Natalie Portman, Samuel L. Jackson and Christopher Lee, their roles in Star Wars will likely define them.

The most heavily involved of the original cast, meanwhile, is Harrison Ford, who does just enough to bind old to new before [redacted]. Mark Hamill makes no showing until the very end, Abrams having foreseen the possibility of his taking over the story (or, the unkind might say, sinking the boat; even without dialogue Hamill's lack of acting prowess is a hole in the making). Carrie Fisher is situated very much on the periphery of events and seems unlikely to feature much in Episodes VIII and IX. All three actors have aged – or to be less facile, haven't been digitally youthened – and a shirty minority of viewers have leapt from this starting point to the conclusion that Fisher, in particular, hasn't aged *well*. What nonsense. It's been thirty-three years since *Return of the Jedi*! One wonders if such puerile fantasists still conceptualise Jane Fonda in her *Barbarella* getup, or Raquel Welsh unchanged since *Fantastic Voyage* and *One Million Years B.C.*? Said viewers might do well to look in the mirror at some point.

Whatever may have been hoped from the original stars in reprise, it seems fair to say (and fingers crossed here that Hamill remains a MacGuffin) that Abrams has used them astutely to usher in a new trilogy where their services are no longer required. With the Disney enterprise now in some measure legitimised, it's time for Star Wars to move on. Certainly this is the case regarding plot, where Abrams and Lawrence Kasdan (co-writer of *The Empire Strikes Back* and *Return of the Jedi*) have retrofitted their screenplay to the point of making it virtually the *new* New Hope. Yes, they've given it some innovative touches – and Kylo Ren's character is an intriguing inversion of what came before – but rightly or wrongly they've spurned the Expanded Universe, while much of what appears on screen is rehashed shamelessly from Episode IV. (And not always to as good effect; evidence: the First Order's overplayed Nazi parade and its ostensibly awesome Starkiller, which ramps up the Death Star concept yet lacks a defining emotive response such as Leia's when Alderaan is destroyed.) This isn't to say the plot is bad or that the new trilogy won't now shoot off in fantastic new directions, but for the time being it seems uncannily as though the Force has awakened on Groundhog Day.

Episode VII is by nature incomplete; unlike *A New Hope*, which had to stand alone, it has been written overtly as the start of a trilogy. Spiritually as well as narratively, however, it comes very much from the mould of Episode IV: a space opera with uncommon substance; a human story unfolding on a grand alien stage; a serious adventure underscored, not undermined, by its humour. Naturally, it isn't perfect – alas, poor Chewie, sent into a berserker rage by [redacted], only minutes later to reappear with a smile at the controls of the *Millennium Falcon* and then stand over with the extras while newcomer Rey shares a hug with Leia – but that was never the hope or expectation. All that fans really wanted was to watch the films in story order and still feel buoyed at the conclusion, not suffer through them in production order, becoming increasingly miffed. To that end it is fingers crossed for the new Star Wars; so far so good and—

Vacuum thump. Orchestral flourish. Credits.

1977 no longer seems quite such a long time ago.

Jacob Edwards

The Visit, by M. Night Shyamalan (Blinding Edge Pictures et al.)

Pop Pop and Nana go gaga as Shyamalan adds another gem to his trove.

Don't cast teens as protagonists. Stay away from twists. Don't try to weave in a message. And please, for the love of all things cinematic, do not use the found footage technique. Such is the advice a critic might bestow upon the director of a contemporary horror film.

Despite ignoring each of these presumed precautions in *The Visit*, M. Night Shyamalan manages to prove his directorial ingenuity once again. The film offers equal parts humour and horror, topped off with Shyamalan's ever-present moral message. And it's all steeped in the scenario that this generation's Hitchcock has mastered: strange things happen to engaging characters in remote and unglamorous locations.

No Cookies and Cocoa

Fifteen-year-old Becca and her peppy younger (by two years) brother Tyler, self-dubbed T-Diamond Stylus, set out to spend a week on their grandparents' Pennsylvanian farm. Becca, a budding director, wants

to film a documentary that explores the longstanding
rift between her mom and her grandparents.

The story, unfolding through Becca's cameras,
quickly reveals that "Pop Pop" and "Nana" are a far cry
from the cookies and cocoa grandparents that many of
us envision... especially when the sun sets. Their
behaviour grows more erratic and more eccentric. The
tight-lipped Pop Pop, prone to bursts of violence,
retreats to his shed and makes the most of his
incontinence. Nana obsesses over the cleanliness of
her oven and engages in a variety of nocturnal
oddities. Employees of the local hospital stop by and
express concern that the couple has stopped coming to
volunteer as counsellors.

By the film's end, the viewer will get gobs of what
Shyamalan does best, such as funny dialogue, the
goosebump-inciting twist, and the evocation of
contrasting emotions. For instance, sequences in
which the siblings debate whether to investigate the
strange sounds just outside their door merge humour
and tension. The film's climax, in which both
protagonists confront their weaknesses, brings to
mind the intensity of that in *There Will Be Blood*.

From Gen Z to Cra-zy
Films with kids who act beyond their years can be
supremely annoying (think *Home Alone*), yet in *The
Visit*, as with other Shyamalan films, it somehow
works. Teens Becca (Olivia DeJonge) and Tyler (Ed
Oxenbould) stand as fully developed characters with
an innocence and sense of wonder that contrasts with
the typical horror film teen so quick to shed clothes
and crack open beers. The siblings also represent
Generation Z. These are the kids who've grown up with
the instant access to unlimited information that
today's technology affords. They're perceptive. They're
intuitive. They're sensitive.

While Becca is the voice of reason, Tyler is the primary source of humour. His vibrancy, curiosity, and even charisma more than make up for his misogynous (Becca's word) impromptu rapping that grows a bit tedious. In one of the funniest scenes, Tyler's bright

green jacket rebels against the bleak winter setting as he imitates Nana's antics.

Though *The Visit* has many strengths, its true jewel is Nana, who bangs and scratches her way through the film. Chicagoan Deanna Dunagan achieves an unpredictability on par with Heath Ledger's Joker: one never knows whether Nana will laugh hysterically or burst into tears and start hitting herself. This instability is especially effective during sit-down interviews when Becca attempts to coax from her grandmother details about the falling out with Becca's mother.

The Revisit
Critics have been unjustifiably harsh with Shyamalan's films. Consequently, it's quite possible that with this latest film about the making of a documentary, Shyamalan is, in a sense, revisiting those critical slings and arrows.

Just as Becca seeks an "elixir" that will heal the wounds between her mother and her grandparents, Shyamalan points to an elixir that could bridge the gap between his oeuvre and its attackers. However, is it possible to find such an elixir? More important, can Pop Pop, Nana, and those critics be trusted? *Douglas J. Ogurek* ★★★★★

Games

Trials Fusion Awesome Max Edition, by RedLynx (Ubisoft)

The Trials series of games are, to the casual glance, so simple that they could have been made on a Spectrum, and, indeed, pretty much were, as fans of Codemasters' *ATV Simulator* will remember. You're just driving a bike along a straight line that sometimes goes up, sometimes goes down, while you lean back and forth to keep it balanced. It's like the old TV show *Kickstart*, except you can't even turn the handlebars. And yet that's just on the surface. The Trials games put that simplest of ideas into a world built with individual objects and subject to physics, where the slightest nudge here or there can make the greatest difference, and where your rider dies horribly at the

end of each level. On some levels it's a thrill ride, hurtling down a snowy mountain like you're chasing James Bond, while on harder levels it's the world's toughest platformer, as you take a hundred attempts to get over one gnarly jump. And since the levels (once you get the hang of them) only take a few minutes to complete, the games are endlessly replayable in search of a better time. This Xbox One expansion of *Trials Fusion* improves upon the Xbox 360 version to the extent that it's well worth a separate purchase. It includes all the DLC, so immediately has an immense range of tracks to ride on, from deserts and ski resorts to various distant, destroyed futures. To cap it all there's a series of incredible levels where you play as a cat riding a unicorn! These were so popular with my children that one suspects an entirely equestrian spin-off could be very popular – they also liked being able to create a female rider for the regular levels. Another improvement is that loading times are much improved. Part of the appeal of *Trials HD* was the way you could rattle through half its levels in a half hour lunch break, something lost in the slovenly Xbox 360 version of this game. The checkpoints in *Trials Fusion* are much closer together than they were in *Trials HD*, making it possible to muddle your way through hard levels in a way that would have been impossible before. At first this seems disappointing, a sop to lightweights, but it's as hard as ever to set a good time, and it's easy to understand why the game's makers would want lots of players to see all of the cool stuff they have created. And for anyone who misses the real teethgrinding challenges of old, the extreme difficulty levels here are as hard as ever – I've yet to pass the first checkpoint in any of them. The game also includes a brilliant local four-player multiplayer mode (allow bailout finishes for maximum fun), a level creator and online game modes, including tournaments where you

post your best time and then wait to see where you came, prizes being awarded to those who reach certain positions. I've yet to mention what a pretty game it is, but it is, and it really shines with the higher definition of a next-generation console. *Stephen Theaker*
★★★★☆

Television

Arrow, Season 2, by Marc Guggenheim and many others (Warner Bros Television)

Oliver Queen was a sleazy rich kid who took his girlfriend's sister away on a disastrous yacht trip, leaving him marooned on an island, from which he was rescued five years later. He returned with a new set of skills, and a new sense of purpose, determined to use his archery and acrobatics to take down the wealthy one percenters who have been bleeding the city dry. Unfortunately, the first season of *Arrow* was in its early stretches often indistinguishable from stablemate *Gossip Girl*, but as its roster of costumed characters built up it improved, an episode with the Huntress attacking her father's compound being particularly good, and it ended well, with a serious threat that pushed the fledgling hero to his limits. Season two is even better, putting Oliver and his night-time *nom de guerre* under an ever-tightening screw, as a friend from the past returns with a grudge. Flashbacks to the island continue, moving more or less in pace with current-day events, creating an unusual effect whereby the viewer must constantly rethink the Oliver we met in the programme's first episode. DC fans will appreciate the introduction of a certain group of villains sent on deadly missions by (the remarkably slim) Amanda Waller, and by the end Black Canary is in it so much they could have put her name in the titles. Supporting characters Diggle and Felicity are also given plenty to do, though Oliver's family and friends, especially his mother and Laurel, tend to zig and zag rather randomly whenever the plot requires it. The season draws on classic *New Teen Titans*, and from there brings us one of the best villains yet in a television superhero series. Despite Felicity's best efforts, there isn't much humour, and the dialogue is rarely more than functional; the thrilling story just about makes up for it, but one hopes John B. Arrowman plays a bigger part in seasons to come. In his few scenes here he displays a totally welcome cheekiness that was rather buried in season one. *Stephen Theaker* ★★★☆☆

Doctor Who, Season 9, by Steven Moffat and friends (BBC)

Peter Capaldi returns for a second season as the Doctor, Jenna Coleman for a third as Clara, and Steven Moffat for his fifth as head writer. Not a surprise then that this feels like the work of people who really know what they are doing with these characters. The Doctor at first is travelling alone, having the party of his life in medieval times because he knows there's trouble up ahead, while Clara is teaching at Coal Hill, where it all began. They are brought back together by Missy, Davros and the Daleks, and by the end of the year they'll have encountered Odin, the Zygons, ghosts in an undersea base, an immortal girl running a sanctuary for aliens, and the creatures that grow from the sleep in your eyes if you leave it unwashed for too long. They'll travel to the very end of the universe and back, while ending every other episode on a cliffhanger.

Though this is a very modern series of *Doctor Who*

in most ways, the special effects, writing, sound design, direction and acting always excellent – I'd say film quality at times, if more films were actually this good – it feels like Steven Moffat's stab at writing a traditional season of the original show: split these episodes in two and you could have five four-part stories, a two-parter, and a six-parter. It's exciting throughout, different again to Moffat's previous seasons, always looking for new ways to test the format, expand its possibilities, and hammer at the Doctor's weaknesses, while also giving children new playground games to play and good advice for life: next season may well focus on the ramifications of the Doctor's mistakes this time around, but an episode in there about the importance of brushing your teeth would be very helpful. And it is immensely generous, leaving galaxies of room for future writers of novels, comics and audio adventures to explore. Moffat's plots wind up into tight little knots, but there's always a thread left for others to follow. That the new programme is still going a decade on is an incredible achievement, that's it's still so brilliant is unbelievable. A credit to everyone who worked on it. *Stephen Theaker* ★★★★★

The Flash, Season 1, by Andrew Kreisberg and many others (Warner Bros Television)

The Flash is a name that has been used by a series of DC Comics characters: Jay Garrick in the forties, Barry Allen from the late fifties, Wally West from the late eighties, and probably a couple more since. The Flash of this television series is Barry Allen, a police scientist who is struck by lightning and becomes the fastest man alive. Before that happened Barry appeared in episodes of *Arrow*, and so, like the forthcoming *Legends of Tomorrow* and *Vixen* animated series this is part of what's sometimes called the Arrowverse. *Gotham* probably isn't a part of this continuity, nor was *Smallville*, nor are any of the planned DC films, but *Supergirl* is in a nearby dimension, and *Constantine* was added after-the-fact once he had appeared in *Arrow*. That's quite the little universe that has grown out of *Arrow*, a show with such unpromising beginnings. *The Flash* gets off to a much better start

than its big brother. The big change from the comics (or at least the comics I've read) is that the lightning storm is brought on by an explosion at STAR Labs, after Harrison Wells turns on his particle accelerator against the advice of his colleagues. This explosion acts much like the meteor crash in *Smallville*, providing an origin for most of the superpowered beings we meet in the programme. (One whose powers don't come from there is Captain Cold, played brilliantly by Wentworth Miller in several episodes.) Wells, along with high-flying assistants Cisco Ramon (Carlos Valdes) and Caitlin Snow (Danielle Panabaker), helps Barry to master his powers, as step by step he becomes the Flash we know and love. Grant Gustin is likeable as Barry Allen, determined to clear his father for the murder of his mother (he saw red and yellow blurs flashing around her in the room that night...), and in love with journalist Iris West, daughter of the police officer who became his guardian once dad was in jail. There is so much to like about the show: its confident handling of story arcs and mysteries, its excellent special effects, the speed with which it builds up a roster of great supporting characters, the diversity of its cast and characters, and how it draws on all the riches of the character's history. This is Barry Allen, but there's a lot of the Wally West stories in here too: fingers crossed for Chunk in season two! For those who have read *Flashpoint*, the risk that this Barry might create that dark universe looms over the season's events. The main villain is properly scary, with his glowing red eyes and readiness to kill. I could live with less mooning over Iris in season two, but the programme originates on The CW so that rather goes with the territory. *Stephen Theaker* ★★★★☆

Notes

Also Received, But Not Yet Reviewed
Notes by Stephen Theaker

Abbott, K.L., *Kindler of Flames*

Adams, Guy, and Jimmy Broxton, *Goldtiger* (Rebellion): from a writer who was my boss at the BFS and an artist who went to the press with allegations that I was corrupt in my administration of the British Fantasy Awards: a two-way conflict of interest!

Bergen, Andrez, *Small Change* (Roundfire Books): a Casebook of Scherer and Miller, investigators of the paranormal and supermundane

Brooks, Robin, *Carmilla* (Audible Originals): adaptation of by J. Sheridan Le Fanu's story, starring Rose Leslie, David Tennant and Phoebe Fox.

Livio Gambarini, *Eternal War – Armies of Saints* (Acheron Books): from a publisher of Italian speculative fiction in the English language.

Loring, Jennifer, *Those of My Kind* (Omnium Gatherum)

Mann, George, *The Osiris Ritual* (Titan Books): a Newbury and Hobbes investigation. Three more titles are forthcoming in the series.

Mills, Pat, Dave Gibbons, and chums, *Dan Dare: The 2000AD Years, Vol. 1* (Rebellion): I've always wanted to read these! My first introduction to both Dan Dare and *2000AD* (and *The Quatermass Experiment*, and *The Thing from Another World*, and many more) was in the *2000AD* Dan Dare quiz book. However, *my* Dan Dare was the one who appeared in the revived *Eagle*.

Morrison, Grant, and others, *The Multiversity* (DC

Comics): this looks magnificent but the resolution of the review pdf is so low that I think it would spoil my first reading of this book.

Petrie, Simon (ed.), *Andromeda Spaceways Inflight Magazine* #61

Tallerman, David, *Patchwerk* (Macmillan-Tor/Forge): newest book from an author who has been kind enough to let us publish his stories a few times; review next issue.

Tidhar, Lavie, *Central Station* (Tachyon Publications)

Weldon, Glen, *The Caped Crusade: Batman and the Rise of Nerd Culture* (Simon & Schuster): new book from a contributor to Pop Culture Happy Hour, one of my favourite podcasts. (Review to appear in *Interzone*.)

About TQF

Copyright

ISBN (print): 978-1-910387-13-9
ISBN (epub): 978-1-910387-14-6

ISSN (print): 1747-6083
ISSN (online): 1747-6075

Website: www.theakersquarterly.blogspot.com

Email: theakersquarterlyfiction@gmail.com

Lulu Store: www.lulu.com/silveragebooks

Feedbooks: www.feedbooks.com/userbooks/tag/tqf

Submissions: Submissions are very welcome! See website for guidelines and terms.

Advertising: We welcome ad swaps with small press publishers and other creative types, and we'll run ads for relevant new projects from former contributors.

Sending material for review: We are interested in reviewing almost anything that's fantasy-related. We prefer to receive books for review in epub or mobi format. Feel free to send ebooks without querying first. We have reviewed about 14% of items received, though many of those reviewed are things we've actively requested from places like NetGalley.

Mission statement: The primary goal of *Theaker's Quarterly Fiction* is to keep going. If you're wondering why we do something a particular way, our primary goal is probably why.

Copyright and legal: All works are copyright the

respective authors, who have assumed all
responsibility for any legal problems arising from
publication of their material. Other material copyright
Stephen Theaker and John Greenwood.

Published in Theaker's Paperback Library
on 26 February 2015.

Other Books

Theaker's Quarterly Fiction #1–53
Stephen Theaker and John Greenwood (eds)

Space University Trent: Hyperparasite
Walt Brunston

There Are Now a Billion Flowers
The Hatchling (forthcoming)
John Greenwood

The Mercury Annual
Pilgrims at the White Horizon
Michael Wyndham Thomas

The Conan Doyle Weirdbook
Rafe McGregor (ed.)

Professor Challenger in Space
Quiet, the Tin Can Brains Are Hunting!
The Fear Man
Howard Phillips in His Nerves Extruded
*Howard Phillips and The Doom That Came to Sea Base
  Delta*
Howard Phillips and The Day the Moon Wept Blood
Stephen Theaker

Five Forgotten Stories
John Hall

Elephant
Harsh Grewal

Elsewhere
Steven Gilligan

New Words #1–4
John Greenwood, Steven Gilligan
and Stephen Theaker (eds)

Forthcoming Attractions

Expect **Theaker's Quarterly Fiction #55** in March.
We're already past the deadline for that one, but feel
free to start sending in submissions for #56.

Our blog is rather more active now:
www.theakersquarterly.blogspot.com

Stephen tweets every few days or so at:
www.twitter.com/Rolnikov

The zine now has its own Twitter account too, though
we keep forgetting the password, so don't expect a
quick reply:
www.twitter.com/TheakersQrtly

Our email address is:
theakersquarterlyfiction@gmail.com

www.ingramcontent.com/pod-product-compliance
Lightning Source LLC
Chambersburg PA
CBHW060812120626
46557CB00001B/184